I0743867

HOW TO CATCH A BACHELOR

SPECIAL EDITION

CHESTER FALLS
BOOK FOUR

ANA ASHLEY

Illustrated by
COVERS BY JULES

How to Catch a Bachelor - Chester Falls Book 4
Original © 2020 by Ana Ashley
Special Paperback Edition: September 2023
ISBN-978-1-915031-08-2

How to Catch a Bachelor is a work of fiction. Names, characters, businesses, places events and incidents are either products of the author's imagination or used in a fictitious manner. Any resemblance to actual persons, living or dead, or actual events is purely coincidental.

Cover design: Covers by Jules

Editor: Alphabitz Editing

Join Ana's Facebook Group *facebook.com/groups/CafeRoMMance* for exclusive content, and to learn more about her latest books at *anawritesmm.com*!

DEDICATION

This book was so much fun to write thanks to the witty
characters of Chester Falls, but I couldn't have done it
without the help of three amazing people.

Tanya and **Lisa** for their endless source of amusement,
support and especially those laugh-out-loud beta comments.

Rhys, for being the best sounding board, whip-cracking,
grammar-policing, cheerleading and motivation I could ever
only dream to have.

Thank You!

ABOUT HOW TO CATCH A BACHELOR

T1ghtBuns: I could knead the best bread you've ever eaten on those tight abs.
TopM4N: *snorts* you sure you're on the right app?

I'm a born romantic.
He doesn't believe in relationships.

Two things we agree on...together we are electric, and we want casual.
We're both **best men** at a wedding, and guess where the bachelor party is?
As they say, **what happens in Vegas, stays in Vegas**...or does it?
Waking up married to an unshakeable bachelor is one thing. Accidentally **falling in love** with him however, is what could get me into real trouble...

How to Catch a Bachelor is the fourth book in the Chester Falls series and features an opposites attract and waking up married tropes, a family with a penchant for inappropriate gifting, lot's of cinnamon buns, and a small town like no other.

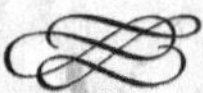

The doorbell dinged. It was already way past closing time, and, as usual, I'd gotten too distracted following my closing routine to lock the door to my coffee shop or even flip the closed sign for that matter.

Not that it would make a difference, because as long as I was out front, there was nothing that would keep my love-sick customers away.

"Hey, Maggie, how's it going?" I asked, not bothering to turn around from where I was behind the counter cleaning the coffee machine. Maggie had come in after-hours every day for the last week suffering from a severe case of seemingly unrequited love. I wasn't so sure it was unrequited but more that the object of her affection was oblivious to her interest.

I heard a deep sigh and plastered the most sympathetic smile I could manage at this time of day before turning around.

"Liam doesn't even know I exist," she said, crossing her arms and pouting.

"Did you speak to him like I suggested?"

Maggie blushed and uncrossed her arms, looking down at the floor.

"Ugh, I'm such a loser. He came in the store and asked if I could fix his rod. I thought he was flirting with me, so I said yes, I'd fix his rod any time. Then he went back to his car and brought out his fishing rod. I literally died."

I had to bite the inside of my cheek so I wouldn't laugh at poor Maggie or point out that since she worked at the fish and tackle shop, Liam's question hadn't been totally out of place.

"So did you, erm...fix his rod?"

"Yes, of course I did." She looked at me like it was the strangest thing to doubt her rod mending abilities.

"Aaand?"

"And then he left."

"Did you make any polite chat or ask him questions?" I asked.

"I tried, but he only answered with yes and no, so after a while I gave up. I know I need to move on from this crush, but I really like him, Indy. The other day I saw him help little Mikey when the chain on his bike came loose. I *literally* melted watching him. He's older, more experienced, and probably would never look at someone like me, but my stupid heart won't stop lusting after him."

She fell on one of the chairs as if she'd lost all hope.

"Oh, Mags." I went around the counter and crouched by her knees, taking her hands in mine. "I don't know Liam very well, but I know what it's like to try to move on after you lose someone. If he's not taking your hints, why don't you try asking him out for a coffee?"

She looked at me with her big blue eyes, a tiny sliver of hope dancing across her pupils.

"What if he says no?" she asked, her voice so little my heart broke for her.

"But what if he says yes?"

Maggie seemed to think about it and made some kind of resolution in her mind. She got up and gave me a hug before leaving.

I took the opportunity to flip the sign to closed and turn the lock on the door, but at that same moment, I saw my friend Ben, the owner of Bookmarked, the only bookstore in Chester Falls, run across the square waving his hand.

"Hey, Indy," he said, out of breath. "Oh jeez, I need to start going to the gym. I'm so out of shape."

"You're saying Tristan doesn't give you good workouts?" I teased.

"Oh, stop it. Not you, too."

I laughed. It was a running joke among our group of friends that whenever Ben and Tristan were in the storeroom at Bookmarked, they were making out because that's how they'd gotten together in the first place.

"How can I help? I know you're not coming to me at this hour for love problems."

He shook his head. "Nope, all good in the love department. In fact, I have some news." Ben paused, his eyes twinkling with happiness.

"Oh my god, he's proposed, hasn't he?" I said, clapping my hands together over my chest.

Ben nodded, and I squealed. I mean, there is only one possible reaction when two of your good friends decide to get married. Squeal. All. The. Way.

"Congratulations. I'm so happy for you two. Have you set a date? I doubt Tristan will want a long engagement."

I gestured for Ben to follow me inside and went around the counter to box up a few cinnamon buns I had left over for him to take home.

"He'd happily go down to the courthouse tomorrow, but he wouldn't dare upset my mom just in case she stops making him his favorite peach cobbler," Ben said.

"Can't blame him. I tried to pry the recipe from her last week, and even after I gave her a box of cupcakes, she still didn't budge."

"That's my mom for you. Anyway, I came over to ask if

you'd like to join us for brunch on Sunday at Benny's," he said. "There's some wedding stuff we'd like to run by you."

"Momma Ruth's blueberry pancakes and wedding talk? Wouldn't miss it for the world."

Ben smiled and then beamed as I gave him the box with his favorite treats.

"My wedding diet will now start tomorrow because Tristan is working late tonight and these babies are going to keep me company," he said, raising the box up to his face, inhaling deeply and rolling his eyes like he'd just taken a hit of his favorite drug.

"Your secret is safe with me," I said with a chuckle, watching as he walked back to Bookmarked. There was a lightness to him since he'd met Tristan, and I couldn't be happier for both of them.

My phone rang just as I locked up and made the short walk up the stairs outside the building to my apartment. Living above my business meant I had to make an extra effort to go out and exercise or walk on my days off, but after closing Spilled Beans, I couldn't deny it was handy not having a commute.

"Hey, Mom, how's it going," I said, toeing my shoes off by the door and answering the call.

"Hi, honey. I'm good, but my fridge is decidedly empty, and I'm definitely not on a diet."

"I will never understand why on earth you'd keep cake inside the fridge."

"Because I like it cold. Besides, it doesn't matter, anyway, because I haven't got any cake, do I?"

I chuckled.

"How about I visit tomorrow and bring you a freshly made one?"

"I would just be happy to see you, honey. You know that."

"Yes, but you'll be happier if I don't turn up empty-handed. Don't pretend that's not the reason you called."

She let out an outraged gasp. "You know me so well. Your dad sends his love."

"Fine, I'll make him a tray of blondies, too."

"Good. I'll make sure to have a pot of your favorite coffee brewing. It's been a while since I grilled you over your love life."

"Mom," I groaned.

"What? A mother can't be interested in her son's happiness?"

"I'm fine, and there's no love life to talk about, so that'll be a very short discussion." I laughed to mask the sudden sinking feeling in the pit of my stomach.

"Indigo, honey, you're not going to wake up married one day."

"I know," I said before we said our goodbyes and ended the call.

I sank into my sofa and looked at the clock on the wall. It was only nine o'clock. For most people, this was the time they were relaxing in front of the TV with a drink or maybe even dinner.

For me, this was bedtime. I was up most days at four to start baking in time to open Spilled Beans with all the fresh treats my customers were now used to.

My schedule and relationships weren't ingredients that went together in the same recipe. I'd slowly come to that realization after all the times I'd started seeing someone regularly only to be dumped when I couldn't have a movie night without falling asleep, go out dancing, or do anything that required being conscious past ten at night.

"Stop it, Indy. No one likes a party pooper. It's the weekend, and for once, you're off work, so dust off the self-pity," I said to myself.

My phone dinged with a message, but what caught my eye as I unlocked the screen was the hookup app that had laid dormant for longer than I cared to remember.

The last message I'd exchanged with someone had a January date stamp. Fuck, had it really been four months since I last got laid? No wonder I was feeling funky.

I removed the elastic band from my hair, leaving it to fall in long waves over my shoulders, and massaged my scalp.

Most of my friends were now all loved up, and as much as I loved seeing them so happy, there was a part of me that was jealous. I also wanted to come home after a long day on my feet to cuddle up to a hard chest and strong arms.

My dick twitched at the thought, so I decided to put it out of its misery and see if there was anyone interesting around.

I scrolled past some of the local guys who were online because I wasn't in the mood for a catch-up. As much as the familiarity of hooking up with someone I already knew was comfortable, tonight, I could do with hard, fast, and anonymous.

"Well, hello, Mr. Washboard Abs. Let me grab my laundry, and I'll be right with you," I said to myself before sending the guy a message and jumping in the shower. Hopefully, soon enough I'd get dirty again.

TATE

T1ghtBuns: I could knead the best bread you've ever eaten on those tight abs.

TopM4N: *snorts* you sure you're on the right app?

Well, color me intrigued. I'd either just been on the end of the best pick up line ever, or I'd been messaged by the most confused baker in a fifty-mile radius.

I looked at his profile while I waited for a reply, which didn't come for fifteen minutes. Fifteen minutes I'd spend staring at the two photos he had on his profile. Fuck me. He couldn't have picked a more suitable nickname than T1ghtBuns.

There were no dick pics. His profile said he was an exclusive bottom, so his money shot was definitely the one with well-worn jeans halfway down the perkiest, tightest bubble butt I'd ever seen. There were no face photos, which wasn't surprising, but the second photo showed long, wavy dark blue hair running down a naked back.

"Come on, T1ghtBuns, don't leave me hanging," I said. My dick filled up at the thought of biting that cute ass and then wrapping my hands around that long hair while I took him from behind.

If T1ghtBuns was a perfect bottom, I was a perfect top, and we were a match made in hot sex heaven.

The app dinged with a message.

T1ghtBuns: *nods* let me proof it to you.
TopM4N: And why would I do that?
T1ghtBuns: Because I'd let you knead my buns in return.
TopM4N: Now we're talking. Can I bring my rolling pin to this party?
T1ghtBuns: It's the yeast you can do.
TopM4N: I am strangely turned on. Also hungry.
T1ghtBuns: Meet me at O'Mahoney's in one hour. I'll bake it worth your while ;)

I laughed out loud at my phone. The last thing I'd expected from today was to score a hookup, but I wasn't one to complain when life handed me ready-to-drink lemonade. And I didn't even need to go far, since O'Mahoney's was a short walk from the motel.

Life really shouldn't be so easy, but once again...lemonade.

TopM4N: Bready or not, here I crumb.
T1ghtBuns: Oh, you will.
TopM4N: *raises eyebrows* and how will I know what you look like?
T1ghtBuns: Don't worry, baby. You won't miss me.

This unexpected turn of events almost made me forget about the rest of my day. *Almost.*

I should know better by now. My day was never over until I was told it was over, as proven by my phone ringing when I'd barely put it down from the brief chat with T1ghtBuns.

My blood pressure went up a few notches, so I took a deep, calming breath and swiped my finger across the screen.

"Mr. Andrews, how can I help?"

"Hey, Brooks. I know you don't mind the late call, so I just wanted to check on the meeting with the Davenports."

Actually, I do mind the late call, especially since I've already given you eighty hours of my life this week. Not that you noticed or even acknowledged my meeting request to talk about my promotion.

"Glad you called, sir. I was actually about to call you myself." *Liar.* "The meeting went better than we could have expected. Mrs. Davenport agreed to a reduction of forty percent of the previously agreed spousal allowance."

"Well done, Brooks. How did you manage that? She seemed hell-bent on screwing the poor man over for every penny he had just because of *that* little indiscretion."

My jaw was so tight I had to take another deep breath and count to five before I replied. *That* little indiscretion was a live-in lover he'd put up in an apartment in the city.

"We managed to convince her that it wouldn't be good for the children if the divorce was dragged through the court." Another deep breath. "And it seems Mr. Davenport's lawyer found new evidence that his wife may not have been completely faithful during their marriage."

"Well, well. The plot thickens, as they say. I'll see you on Monday."

"Have a good weekend, sir."

It was a good thing I was already headed to the shower because I needed to wash this fucking day off, and then if I played my cards right, I'd be fucking T1ghtBuns well into tomorrow morning.

Thirty minutes later, I sat at the bar in O'Mahoney's with a cold beer in hand. The place was packed, and not for the first time, I wondered how I was going to identify my date for the night.

Sitting at the bar was a great way to eavesdrop on people's conversations while I waited. So far, I'd found out that this was the only gay bar for miles. There was a mix of regulars who hooked up with each other, and then what they called fresh meat.

Based on how many times I'd been approached, I gathered I'd been well and truly identified as fresh meat.

I'd kept my eye on the door, waiting, scanning each guy that came in. So far, none had piqued my interest, and all had gone straight to other guys they clearly knew well.

I took a final sip of my beer and looked at my phone. There were no messages from T1ghtBuns. He said to meet him in one hour, so he wasn't late yet, but my curiosity about him was making me even more eager to know what he looked like, especially after our chat.

A new guy by the door definitely caught my attention this time. Tall, although I couldn't tell from where I sat if he was taller than me, dark hair tied in a bun with a few loose strands that framed his beautiful face perfectly, a tight t-shirt that showed toned arms, and a roaming eye.

Both my dick and I prayed this was my guy because fuck me, he was hot and couldn't be more my type if I'd ordered him from a catalog.

A big guy approached him and whispered something into his ear. He smiled, whispered something back to the other, and gave him a kiss on the cheek. The big guy hugged my guy and left to join his friends.

Okay, he wasn't my guy, but he was going to be if T1ght-Buns didn't turn up soon.

My heart skipped a beat when his eyes met mine. His smile was warm and friendly.

Please, god, let this be my guy. I'll do my own filing for a week.

As quickly as his smile reached his eyes, whose color I couldn't decipher from a distance, it disappeared to give way to a frown. Then he turned on his heels and went toward the bathroom.

My phone buzzed only seconds later.

T1ghtBuns: Hey, I'm at O'Mahoney's. I'll look for you in a bit. Just need to take care of something first.
TopM4N: Sure thing Sweet Buns.
T1ghtBuns: How do you know my buns are sweet?
TopM4N: A guy knows these things. Go deal with your business, then come find me. I'll be the hot guy fighting off the locals. Might need to be rescued.

I waved at the barman to grab his attention, but my hand stopped mid-wave when the stunning guy from the door sat next to me.

Up close, he was breathtaking. So much so that I almost did forget to breathe.

His hair had looked dark from a distance, but in the brighter lights of the bar, I could tell it had a dark blue color to it. His eyes were also a deep, dark shade of blue. Had he dyed his hair to match his eyes?

"Please tell me you're T1ghtBuns," I said, eager to find out if there really was a god and that she loved me.

The guy's eyes widened ridiculously, and he opened his mouth like he was in shock or something.

"You're...TopM4N?"

"The one and only. Can I get you a drink?"

"How could you do this to him?" he asked.

Huh?

"Do what to whom?"

"Your boyfriend, or shall I say *fiancé*, is at home thinking you're working late, and you're at a bar picking up strangers you met through a hookup app?"

Wait...oh, I know what you're doing. Game on, baby.

"What he doesn't know won't hurt him, right?" I said,

shifting in my seat to move closer to him. "How about we take this party somewhere real private where no one can tell on us?"

I'd barely finished speaking when his hand landed on my face with a sharp slap. *What the fuck?*

The three seconds it took me to recover were enough to see the back of the guy as he all but ran toward the door.

I chased after him, catching up when he stopped to open the door to his car.

"Wait, what's wrong? I thought this is what you wanted," I said.

"When did I ever give you the impression I'd betray one of my best friends?"

I put my hand over the door of the car to stop him from leaving.

"Okay, stop," I said. He turned around and crossed his arms over his chest. "We were role-playing, right? I mean...I thought we were, weren't we?"

"Role-playing?" His eyes narrowed, and I noticed the little creases on his forehead. Somehow, they made him even cuter. *Focus, Brooks.*

"Yes. You know, when you come into a bar pretending to catch the other person cheating and then you have angry sex."

"What the fuck is wrong with you, Tristan? Who the fuck does that? I'm going to drive home and forget tonight happened. I don't know if you've done this before, but I suggest you come clean to Ben, or I will. He's a good guy, and he doesn't deserve what you're doing to him."

I waited until his rant was over, biting the inside of my cheek to stop me from smiling because I could tell it wouldn't go down well with this guy.

"Tristan as in...Tristan Brooks?"

"Yes, I believe that's your name. Are you on some kind of drugs?" He leaned forward to look right into my eyes.

That time I did laugh.

"No, I'm not on any drugs. But I'm also *not* Tristan Brooks."

He waved his hand in front of my face, and I took it, placing a small kiss on the back before he took it away as if my touch was cursed.

"Tate Brooks. Tristan's better looking and older by ten minutes twin brother."

INDY

My hand felt like it burned from the kiss. Maybe that's what happened when you cheated on your best friend with his fiancé. It would probably fall off now, and I'd have to learn how to bake one-handed.

No, I hadn't done anything wrong. He was the one who was trying to get away with cheating. I fucking hated cheaters.

"This is a sick game you're playing, Tristan."

"I'm. Not. Tristan," he said, drawing out each word as he inched closer, leaving me trapped between him and my car.

There was a half-smile on his lips, and I noticed a tiny beauty mark just above his top lip. You almost couldn't see it under his beard. Damn it, if I could see that, he was too close.

I pushed him back and said, "If you're not Tristan, then why didn't you...um...he tell me he had a twin brother?"

He shrugged and pulled his wallet from the back pocket of his slacks, taking out his driver's license and showing it to me.

I took it from him for inspection. Tate Brooks.

Whatever the color of mortification was, it was probably the same as my face right about now.

"So, I've told you my name. What's yours? And more importantly, since we're establishing that I am not, in fact, my brother, can we go back to that part of the hookup where we...you know, hookup?" he said.

I shook my head, still trying to get around the fact Tristan had a twin brother who was also gay, and clearly not fazed by hooking up with one of his brother's friends.

"I'm, um...I'm Indy." I thrust my hand in his direction, and he took it.

"Is that short for Indiana?"

"Indigo," I said, looking at our joined hands where his thumb was caressing my skin and leaving a small trail of tingles.

"Of course it is."

His warm voice pulled me in like honey and whiskey. The tingles from my hand spread through my body, settling in the pit of my stomach. If I didn't know any better, I'd think I was drunk.

"We can't hookup," I blurted, pulling my hand back.

"Why not?" he asked, tilting his head.

"Because you're my friend's brother, and until ten seconds ago, I thought you were him."

"I'll make you a deal. We can forget about the hookup...for now...if you share the contents of that box. I've been promised a good time, so I'm collecting."

I looked behind me to the box with the muffins and cinnamon buns I'd brought with me. It had been a last-minute thought when I was getting ready earlier, but however weird it was to bring pastries to a hookup, I'd drawn the line at taking them inside the bar.

"They're actually for you," I confessed, suddenly feeling a little embarrassed.

He leaned against the car, still far too close to me, and crossed his arms before saying, "You brought baked goods to a hookup."

"Yeah...well, the baking puns from our chat. I thought it

would be funny. There are some muffins and a couple of cinnamon buns."

"Where did you find them this late?"

"I made them. I own a coffee shop and had these left over from today."

Tate went around to the other side of the car, opened the passenger door, and grabbed the box. Then he walked back and pulled me by the hand toward a path on the side of the bar.

"Where are we going?" I asked, trying to pull my hand back and locking my car from the short distance we'd walked.

"Motel next door."

"What?"

"Don't worry; your virtue is safe with me."

"My virtue?" I snorted as we turned a corner. "You saw half of my ass on my profile photos. I think it's safe to say my virtue is not very...virtuous."

He turned to look behind me at my ass. "You have a very nice virtue. Shame I won't be tapping that tonight. Still, I bet these are the second best offer I'll have all night," he said, raising the box to his face to smell it.

"Damn right, they are."

The good thing about my body clock and being used to waking up early was that it always allowed me to slip away from a hookup unnoticed. Not that I'd hooked up with Tate. No. Noooo.

Okay, so maybe I fell asleep on him after eating a muffin *and* a cinnamon bun. Everyone knows you shouldn't mix your sugars.

Oh god, did I say yes when he proposed to me?

He didn't propose for real, of course. He was suffering from sugar-induced hallucinations, and if I had a dollar for each person that asked me to marry them after eating one of my bakes, I'd be rich and very not single.

By five in the morning, I was already home and showered, and by nine, I was pulling my dad's blondies out of the oven, with my mom's cake cooling on the rack to the side.

Despite the shorter-than-usual night and the hour drive back from the motel to Chester Falls, I was still as perky as usual. Jake, who was my only full-time employee, had a theory that I got high on flour and sugar. He was probably right.

"You do know how days off work, right?" Jake said, coming into the kitchen to fill a tray with cookies to take out front.

"I'm going to visit my parents today. You know their love is conditional."

He snorted. "Yeah, on the condition you bring cake."

It was more of a running joke than the truth because I loved baking for my parents. They'd championed my love of baking for as long as I could remember.

They were at the front of the queue on the opening day of Spilled Beans and would talk about my cakes and pastries to anyone that gave them more than three minutes of their time.

Today I was hoping the cakes—and the additional cookies I made for my younger brother—would be enough of a distraction so that they'd skip talking about my personal life and talk about what was going on in their hippie community.

I always loved to hear about the new family that would move into the neighborhood only to realize that in the summer, the residents often forgot to wear clothes. Or the street parties where everyone was invited and the mini-festival they organized for the kids to end the summer holidays and start the school term with good energies.

If I thought I'd get away with avoiding questions about my love life, I clearly didn't know my mother and her intuitive powers very well.

"Good morning, sweetheart," she said, taking the cake

boxes from my hands and putting hers straight in the fridge before she came over to give me a hug.

"I hope you know that the depth of my love for you is negatively correlated by how much it hurts me to see you put fresh cake in the fridge."

She gave me a good squeeze that took my breath away before she took her own coffee blend out of the freezer. I didn't know what was in it, and she'd never give the secret away, but her coffee was the best I'd ever had.

"Are you going to let me stock your coffee at Spilled Beans one day? My customers would go wild for it," I said, taking a seat at the table in the large family kitchen.

"You know this blend is special and just for you. How else would I guarantee you'd visit me?"

"Oh shush, you see me plenty."

"So...who is this new guy you're seeing?"

Fuck.

"What are you talking about? I'm not seeing anyone."

I didn't know why my voice had suddenly taken a pre-pubescent high pitch, because I was telling the truth. I wasn't seeing anyone. Even my hookup last night had been a failure.

She finished brewing the coffee and poured it into two cups before placing one in front of me.

Her voice was calm, almost like it gained an ethereal energy, as she said, "I'm sensing a change in the wind. It's going to cause you to shift a little. Maybe you'll feel off-center for a while, but it'll be good. Sometimes we need a good blow."

I snorted. "You did not just say that to me."

"Indigo Moonlight Birch," she chided.

"I'm sorry, Mama. There's no one. Honestly."

She looked at me with her dark blue eyes, the same color as mine, as if she was trying to see into my soul. My mom was never wrong when she listened to her intuition.

Was it possible that I was going to meet someone who'd

fall in love with me until we were so old and would only eat cake because we had no teeth?

She put her hand on mine and squeezed gently.

"He's out there, sweetheart. And who knows? Maybe the new spring breeze will blow him toward you."

"Mom, I promise I'll believe you, but please stop saying the word blow."

After our chat, I found my dad at the end of their garden painting and spent some time with him and then my brother before I drove back to Chester Falls.

On the drive home, I thought about my mom's words. A small shiver of anticipation ran down my spine.

Then the image of Tate licking his lips after taking his first bite of my cinnamon bun made its way into my head.

No. Noooo. No!

TATE

I'd always been an early riser and was also a fairly light sleeper, which was why I was surprised to wake up this morning to find out I'd been out-ninja'd by the cute baker with the dark blue hair.

When we'd got to my motel room last night, the first thing Indy did was to remove his shoes and the hairband that held his hair up before I'd even closed the door behind us.

I'd gone to the bathroom to change into a t-shirt and sweatpants and came out to find Indy sitting cross-legged in the middle of the bed with the cake box open and looking so relaxed it was as if he'd found his way home instead of my motel room.

Indy's cakes turned out to be the best I'd ever had in my entire life, but I wasn't sure I enjoyed them as much as I did flirting shamelessly with him. Indy, on the other hand, had stood his ground and refused to engage with my flirting, deciding instead to eat the other half of the pastries and talk about literally anything else but the reason that had brought us to the same place last night.

I knew I wasn't going to push anything with him. He

seemed freaked out by how much I looked like Tristan, but fuck if I hadn't enjoyed teasing him.

Somehow it was decided he would spend the night even though we hadn't actually had the conversation. In his cake-fueled, relaxed state, he'd ended up falling asleep, and I hadn't had the heart to send him away.

Okay, so maybe I'd spent some time watching him sleep with his long wavy hair sprawled over my pillow. And maybe I pushed some of the hair away from his face so I could have a better look.

Either way, when I woke up this morning, I was on my own in bed, and the space next to me was cold.

Maybe he dreaded the morning-after conversation as much as I did and decided to save us both the awkwardness. It didn't stop me thinking about him, even as I pulled up to park by the book store owned by my brother's boyfriend.

Not boyfriend. Fiancé.

The store looked old fashioned from the outside with a quirky wooden sign hanging by the door with the store name, Bookmarked.

Inside, the store was busy. There was a guy behind the checkout desk serving a line of customers. He had dark-rimmed glasses and wore a t-shirt that said *Books are my jam* with a picture of a book between two slices of bread. That had to be Ben.

He was cute in a nerdy kind of way, and I could see from how he smiled and talked to his customers why he'd caught my brother's attention. He'd always had a soft spot for nice people.

I started browsing the romance aisle, which seemed to be by far the biggest section in the store.

"Don't you just love gay romance?" an older woman said as she picked up a book off the shelf. "Who knew reading about two men falling in love would be so... tantalizing."

She put her hand on my arm, which was when I realized she was talking to me and not herself.

"Of course, some of us get to live out our own romance story, right? You're a lucky man." Her eyes darted over to where Ben was working his queue of customers.

"Oh no, I'm not..."

The woman waved her hand and left to join the line.

Twenty minutes later, I'd given up trying to explain to people that I wasn't Tristan and just went with it. I picked up a trolley that had books that needed returning to the shelves and started working through them. Where the hell was my brother, anyway?

"Hey, the new kid is here, *finally*. Wanna come to the storeroom and *not* help me with a deliv..."

I turned around to face Ben, and he stopped mid-sentence, narrowing his eyes as if he was trying to figure out what was wrong with me.

"Oh my god, Tate, you're here," he said excitedly. It was as if he wanted to give me a hug but was trying to contain himself.

"According to the last five customers I helped, I'm Tristan, so give me a minute to check my ID because even *I'm* confused right now," I said.

He chuckled. "Tristan is here all the time, and you look so much like him," Ben said, smiling. "I mean, I can tell you're not him now but not when you were facing the other way."

"We get that a lot. And now I know your romance customers love friends to lovers stories, but there's an old lady who has to be at least a hundred years old and is into daddy kink."

"That's Sophia. She's eighty-five going on thirty and started reading gay romance last year. I'm sure she's single-handedly responsible for the success of my LGBT romance section."

I wasn't so sure about that considering how many people of all ages I'd seen browsing that particular section.

"Do you want to come upstairs? Tristan said he'd grab us some coffee and pastries from Spilled Beans. He'll be happy that you're here already. I was hoping to take the afternoon off, but it's busy, so I'm going to take a short break and leave you two to catch up."

I followed Ben through a door that led to an apartment above the store, which was where he and my brother lived.

"It's so nice to finally meet you. Tristan talks about you all the time," Ben said.

I laughed. Tristan and I were as close as we could be growing up, but we were separated when our parents divorced. Seeing each other during the school vacations wasn't the same as living under the same roof, so we drifted apart, and it wasn't until we left for college that we reconnected.

Our relationship had never regained the same closeness, but I was happy that we were on speaking terms, something I couldn't say for my relationship with our dad, especially now our mom was gone.

"I wish I could say the same about you, but I guess that's why I'm here this weekend. Tell me about you and your store."

Ben smiled and looked at a photo he had hanging up on the wall of an older woman and a younger-looking Ben.

"Bookmarked was my aunt's store. She left it to me when she died, and I've been managing it ever since."

"It was pretty busy downstairs earlier. A cute store like this would make a killing in the city. Have you considered expanding? Maybe opening a store in Boston?"

"No, I'm really not a city person. I moved back here from Boston after college and have no desire to get back. Besides, I love Chester Falls. I love knowing all my customers, what they like to read, and I love that at Bookmarked, everyone has a space to hang out and expand their horizons all without leaving the safety of the store."

"You have to keep your options open, Ben. You never know what tomorrow holds."

He stared at me as though I was speaking a foreign language.

Fuck, did I offend him?

And this was why I didn't see my brother more often. Most of my friends were attorneys, so talking business was a form of relaxation in itself, especially for me because I was exhausted from divorce law and was dying for the chance to do something else.

"Hey, old man," my brother said, coming into the small apartment holding three coffees and the promised pastry bag.

"Hey, kiddo," I replied.

Tristan gave Ben his coffee and a look that was so full of promise it was as if they'd had a full-on conversation.

I'd seen those looks many years ago between my parents. That was, of course, before it all went wrong.

"So, what have you been talking about?" he asked.

"Nothing much. Only that Ben agrees I'm definitely hotter than you," I said, stealing the pastry bag from him.

Tristan laughed. "Hardly."

I would have retaliated, but the sweet scent of cinnamon took me right back to last night when I'd been so close to Indy, watching him sleep, and I could smell both his shower soap and a lingering scent of cake batter. I'd wondered then if he always smelled like that.

"Where did you get these?" I asked.

"Spilled Beans just across the square. They have the best pastries in the world."

I looked out of the window, wondering if somehow Fate's twisted sense of humor had brought me close to Indy again.

Little did I know how twisted Fate's sense of humor *really* was.

INDY

I loved visiting my parents, but being grilled about my non-existent love life was part of our routine, even if I dreaded it every time.

In the same way a lot of people started conversations with the weather, with my parents, it was all about getting an update on when I would be able to give them grandchildren or live the same love story they had. The order in which they occurred wasn't important.

My brother always joked about our lives being a computer game with different levels.

Go on more than one date with the same person, win a special demon-slaying weapon.

Declare that you're in a committed relationship, go up a level.

Introduce a boyfriend to the family, extra points and an additional spell.

Move in together, go up another level.

I didn't like to think too often about the one time when I almost won the game. Nowadays, when my mother's super intuition kicked in and gave me silly ideas, I always felt a little on edge, so despite not getting much sleep over the last two days, I was still up early. And when I was restless like this, there was only one thing that helped.

I lucked out when I opened my cupboards to find I had all the ingredients to bake Ben's favorite cookies—chocolate chip and pecan. At least I wouldn't be told off by Jake again for going down to Beans on my day off.

A few hours later and with a box of cookies in my hand, I stepped into Benny's, feeling a lot more relaxed and looking forward to hearing all about Ben and Tristan's wedding plans.

Ben was in a booth by himself, so I waved at Benny, who was behind the counter looking as happy as I'd ever seen him and joined my friend.

"Hey," I said, sitting opposite him with my back to the door. "Where's Tristan? No, don't tell me. You spent the weekend in bed, and now the poor guy is exhausted and can't even make it to eat Momma Ruth's pancakes."

He had the decency to blush, but then said, "He's on his way. But...you're not entirely wrong."

"I made you these as a happy engagement present." I gave him the box. "You might need them for energy."

Ben opened the box and squealed when he saw the cookies. I was pleased with how they came out. Even from where I sat, the smell of the chocolate chips made my mouth water.

"Damn, I'd marry you if I wasn't engaged already," he said.

"And in love with someone else."

"Meh, details. These cookies are worth a loveless marriage."

"But not good enough to break up the engagement. I see where my cookies come in the pecking order. Don't come crawling to me begging when you're tired of all the awesome sex."

"It'll be my burden to carry," Ben said with an exaggerated sigh.

"I'll light a candle for you," I joked, picking up a menu to see what today's special pancakes were.

"They're here," Ben said.

I caught the ridiculous smile on his face before I turned around to greet Tristan. My stomach sank, and I didn't need a mirror to know all the color had drained from my face when I saw he wasn't alone.

There, in a pair of hot as fuck jeans and a shirt with the sleeves rolled up to his forearms, was Tate. The Tate who wasn't Tristan. The Tate whose bed I'd slept in two nights ago. Tristan's twin brother Tate.

They stopped to greet Benny, which I hoped would give me a minute to get my heart rate back to normal, or plan my escape.

"I know exactly what you're thinking," Ben said, chuckling.

"What? What do you mean?" I asked, spinning my head round to Ben so fast it made me dizzy.

"They're like the same person, right? Yesterday I nearly propositioned him because I thought he was Tristan when he was at Bookmarked. I knew Tristan was a twin, but I didn't know how similar they looked," Ben said.

"Oh, um, yeah. They look...yeah..."

What was the etiquette for meeting a hookup in a social situation? Did we pretend we didn't know each other? How much would Tristan hate me if he found out I'd slept with his brother?

You're going to give yourself an aneurysm, Indigo. Nothing happened the other night.

"Morning, Indy," Tristan said, taking a seat next to Ben, which gave Tate no option but to sit next to me. "This is my twin brother, Tate."

I had to give Tate credit for giving me a polite smile that gave nothing away.

"Hi. Nice meeting you. Indy, right?" he said, stretching out his hand, and sitting closer to me. "Is that Indy for Indiana?" His question took me back to the bar parking lot two nights ago when I thought he was Tristan.

Have the seats shrunk? Why is he so fucking close?

"Indigo," I said, holding out my hand and keeping the handshake brief. I pulled it back quickly so I could hold the menu. You totally needed two hands, especially at Benny's, because they always have so much on offer. It's not like I've eaten here so many times that I've committed most of it to memory. Not at all.

Tate looked at my hair and smiled. "Of course. Indigo. So what's good in this place?"

"Pancakes," said both Ben and Tristan.

"Hmm, there are some interesting options," he said while leafing through the menu.

"How about you, Indy? What's your favorite thing?"

I looked at Tate, who was staring back at me with his piercing blue eyes. From the corner of mine, I could see that Ben and Tristan were absorbed in each other, going through the pancake options.

"Momma's Breakfast," I said, reaching out and pointing at his menu. It wasn't the best move because suddenly we were pressed too close together, and the awareness coursing through my body was making me dizzy.

Serves you right for having cookies for breakfast.

"French toast stuffed with vanilla cream filling and served with fresh fruit," he read out loud. "Sounds good, but I'm sure it won't be as good as those cinnamon buns I had yesterday."

I snapped my head in his direction. At this rate, I was going to give myself a neck injury.

He tilted his head. That smile he had when I'd first approached him at the bar was back. This was dangerous territory because now, with Tristan right here, I could definitely tell the difference between them. Yup, there was no way I'd ever confuse them again.

"What? What do you mean?" I snapped.

Tristan looked up and said, "Oh, yeah. I got to Spilled

Beans yesterday just in time to grab the last few buns before Jake sold out."

"Oh, right, of course. Jake did leave me a message saying we'd sold out earlier than normal."

"Did you make those?" Tate asked as if he hadn't had the same pastries the night before.

"Yeah, I own Spilled Beans, the coffee shop across the square from Bookmarked."

"You must be very good with your hands," he said. "Those buns were delicious."

I coughed and straightened up in my seat, taking the chance to bump my knee against his as a silent plea.

He seemed to have received the message because he shifted his attention to Momma Ruth when she came over to take our order, flirting so shamelessly with her that I was surprised Benny didn't come over to mark his territory.

As soon as we all had our coffee cups full, I raised mine in a toast.

"Ben, Tristan, I'm so happy for you and the news of your engagement. I know you're going to have a very happy and long life together."

I thought I heard a snigger coming from Tate, but when I looked at him, his face showed as much emotion as a flat cake.

Fortunately, Ben and Tristan were looking at each other so adoringly I didn't think they noticed, so I completed my little speech.

"I would be very honored if you accept your wedding cake as a gift from me."

I wasn't expecting fireworks, but maybe just a little more excitement than the awkward smile Ben threw my way.

"Um, I don't have to bake it. I'd be happy paying for it if you already have someone else in mind," I said quickly.

"Oh no, it's not that, Indy," Tristan said.

"We'd be so happy if you could make the cake, but we'll

pay for it," Ben said. "We wouldn't want to put something else on you as well."

"I don't understand," I said.

Ben smiled a hopeful smile and said, "Indy, Tate, the reason we asked you both here today is because we want you both to be our best men."

I clutched my hands in front of my mouth and had to bite on them to stop from squealing.

"Are you serious?" I asked.

They both nodded.

"Oh my gosh, I'd be so happy. But wait...I thought you'd pick Ellie. She's your best friend," I said.

"I spoke to Ellie already. She'd love to be my best man...or woman, but she's just had Charlotte, so she's busy being a mommy. It was actually her suggestion that I pick you."

I got up to give Ben a hug over the table. "I'd love to be your best man, *and* I'm still making your cake because I don't believe for one second that Ellie will be on the sidelines watching."

Ben laughed. "Yeah, I think you're right."

It wasn't until I sat back down that my brain picked up that second detail I seemed to have missed the first time around. Tate was Tristan's best man.

TATE

*B*est man? Me? Tate Brooks? A best man?

The only thing I could think that I was *best at* was being an attorney, and even then, I was a divorce attorney. Who'd want a divorce attorney for a best man?

"So what do you say?" my brother asked.

"About what?"

"Being my best man." He paused for just a second, and I didn't like the doubt I saw in his eyes. "I know things haven't always been easy for us, but we're grown up now. We can take our relationship back, and I'd like to start by having you back in my life."

I knew he was right, but it was because I wanted our relationship back so much that I was afraid I'd screw things up.

Maybe I just needed to figure out a way to do the right things. That's what the internet is for, right?

"I guess you're right, and you're also warned, I'm going to be the worst best man ever," I said.

Tristan laughed.

"Here's your food, boys. Let me know if I can getcha anything else or coffee refills, alright?" Benny said.

I cut through my french toast, scooping as much of the vanilla cream as possible before I put it in my mouth.

"Hmm, this is delicious," I said, taking another forkful and piercing through some of the strawberries. "Hey, Momma Ruth, I don't suppose you're looking for a second husband, are you?"

"You couldn't keep up with me, boy," she shouted back from behind the counter.

I laughed, noticing how Indy was trying not to smile, so I elbowed him.

"I bet you wouldn't have the guts to ask her to marry you," I teased.

"November 2, 1990," Ben said, and Indy groaned.

"What happened?" I asked.

Indy's face went red, and he looked like for once he wished his hair was down to cover it.

"That was the day Indy asked Momma Ruth if he'd marry her when he grew older because she gave him a free stack of blueberry pancakes and it was his birthday."

Benny seemed to have turned up out of nowhere with a fresh pot of coffee.

"No one's taking my Ruth from me. Even you young boys with your six-packs and fancy hair," he said pointedly at Indy. "Besides, she likes a little more man on her man." He patted his belly and finished refilling our coffee cups before he went back behind the counter.

The food was great, the coffee strong, and the people were...interesting. I could see why my brother had decided to move to this small town.

"So, when's this wedding, anyway?" I asked.

"We haven't got a date yet," Ben said. "Well, we haven't decided on a lot of things. It's all still new."

The blush on his face was kind of adorable, and the way he looked at my brother tugged at strings I didn't know my heart had.

"How about early September?" Tristan said.

"Isn't that too early?" I asked. "I mean, don't people stay engaged for some time before the actual wedding?"

Indy shifted in his seat and hit my leg with his again. Without taking my eyes off Ben or my brother, I placed my hand on Indy's knee. He tried to take it away, but I gripped it tighter.

My brother carried on. "I guess some people do, but there's no reason to wait. Besides, early September is Jackie's birthday, and I think it would be a nice celebration for her favorite nephew to marry on her birthday."

"Do you mean that?" Ben asked, looking at my brother like he'd hung the moon.

I turned to Indy to give the love birds a moment because I wasn't sure which one was going to turn into paper hearts and fly away first, Ben or Tristan.

"So, what other delicious things can you do with your hands?" I said, keeping the grip on his leg, but moving my hand up his thigh under the table.

"I um...I do cupcakes..."

Indy's Adam's apple bobbed up and down. His eyes burned with desire, even though his body was trying to say otherwise. I eased up my grip but didn't completely remove my hand until it brushed past his dick.

His breath caught, and then he looked at me with a murderous gaze that wrapped around my balls like a vice.

Was thirty-one a good age to discover a new kink? Because between those delicious buns, sinful lips, and intense eyes, I was starting to think Indy was it.

I'd been hard ever since I'd arrived at the diner to see my hookup escapee sitting with my brother's fiancé. For a moment, I'd contemplated making a joke, but his expression told me he preferred to keep his after-hours activities private, and I respected that.

"It's decided then. September tenth, if we can find an officiant to marry us on that day."

Ben's words cut through my lust haze to bring me back to the reason I was a hundred and forty miles away from home.

"Great," Indy said, scooting closer and pushing me to get out of the booth. "I'm really sorry guys, but I just remembered I have a big cupcake order for Tuesday and could do with starting on the decorations today so I'm not rushing."

He didn't give me a choice but to get up or I'd be pushed until my ass was on the floor.

"Come by Beans this week, and we'll talk about your cake. I already have some ideas swirling in my head, but I'd love to get your intake first."

When he turned to leave, he managed to stop a mere inch short of bumping into me. His brows were furrowed and his eyes were down as he sidestepped to walk around me.

Shit, was he angry because I teased him earlier? Did I take it too far?

I pulled enough money out of my wallet to cover for the food and dropped it on the table.

"I'm going to catch up with my best man sidekick before I head to Boston. I'll call you later, okay?"

"Sure," Tristan said. "It was good to see you, old man."

I chuckled. "It was good to see you, too, kiddo. You know this one is way out of your league, right?" I said to my brother, and pointing at a blushing Ben.

He put his arm around his fiancé to pull him closer and then looked at me. Something from deep within tugged at me. Tristan and I had that twin connection when we were kids, but then we lost it.

Now, the way his eyes bore into my soul, it was as though he could see something in me I couldn't see myself. It was disconcerting, so I gave him a light punch on the shoulder and left.

I looked around the parking lot to find Indy and saw him

approaching his car. I picked up my pace and caught up to him just as he opened the door.

"Hey, Tight Buns."

He turned and looked around, probably to make sure no one had heard me.

"What's up?" he said, looking uncomfortable.

"Did I do or say something that upset you?"

"You know exactly what you were doing." His voice was clipped as he removed the hairband from his hair. His long fingers ran through it and re-tied his bun with the skillful dexterity of someone who's been doing it for years. I suspected it was something he did to keep his hands busy rather than a real need to redo his hair.

Fuck if that wasn't the sexiest thing I've ever seen a man do.

So, I guess you're into man buns now. Great.

"From what I could gather, you were enjoying it," I said, looking down at the bulge in his jeans.

His eyes snapped back to mine. That dark blue going darker. I couldn't help smiling, because there was an equal chance he was angry or turned on, so I carried on testing the waters.

"Besides, we're going to be best men together. We have, what, six months to give the love birds the best wedding they could ever have? And..." I ran my eyes slowly up and down Indy's slim frame, appreciating every inch. "If we have some fun ourselves, it's a bonus. I mean, it's in the rule book, right?"

"The what?"

"The rule book. You know, the wedding rule book," I said, getting closer and tucking a loose strand of wavy hair behind his ear.

Indy closed his eyes and leaned his face gently into my hand.

I leaned in, my lips so close to his I could almost taste them, and said, "Aren't best men meant to hook up? We're already halfway there, Indigo. I'm already *hooked*, if you're *up* for it."

His hands came up to fist my shirt, and I was certain he was going to pull me down for a kiss. Or maybe it was wishful thinking because those lips hadn't left my mind ever since I'd seen them wrapped around a cinnamon bun two nights ago.

Instead, he pushed me away so fiercely I nearly tripped.

"No. There will be no hookups. This," he said, pointing between us, "is going to be a strictly professional relationship until my friends have their dream wedding. Got it?"

"Uh-huh." I nodded.

"Good. You know where to find me if you need me."

And with those parting words, Indy left me in the middle of Benny's parking lot alone with my raging hard-on. It was going to be a long drive to Boston.

INDY

$\mathcal{M}$oaning was always a good sign, and so were eyes rolled so far back in pleasure they were almost closed.

"Shall I leave you alone with it?" I chuckled. "I kinda feel like a pervert watching you make those sounds."

"Fuck, Indy. This cake is delicious," Ben said, putting his fork down on the plate.

"You said that about the last four."

"No, I said the chocolate one was orgasmic, and that one is definitely in."

"Do you want to consult your fiancé?"

"Nope. If he doesn't agree with me, I'm ordering two wedding cakes and he'll just have to watch me eat mine all on my own."

I didn't doubt Ben would do that for a second. While his all-time favorite pastry was my cinnamon buns, his preferred cake was chocolate. Even when he said he wanted to try something different, it just meant that he'd have chocolate and orange, or chocolate hazelnut, rather than plain chocolate.

"Do you want me to tell you about the cakes?" I asked. Normally, brides or grooms-to-be wanted to learn how I combined my flavors. That also came with them telling me the story of how they met or how the proposal went. It was one of my favorite parts of the job. I was a sucker for a love story.

"I'll wait for Tristan."

"Wait...you're saying Tristan is coming..."

"Yup."

"And you started tasting the cake... without him."

"He promised to love me forever." He shrugged as if Tristan's love declaration was his get-out clause for everything, including a head start on cake tasting.

I cut two new slices of each cake and lined them up neatly on clean plates. I'd be surprised if Ben had second servings, but just because this was a cake tasting for friends, it didn't mean I wouldn't make an effort.

If anything, I'd gone over and beyond in my research for the best combinations for my two friends. I wanted them to remember the flavor of their wedding for the rest of their lives.

"Now keep your hands off these ones. We're waiting for Tristan," I warned as I placed the plates on the table.

Ben raised his hands and then crossed them over his chest.

"So, how's things with you?" he asked.

"What do you mean?"

"You ran out of the diner pretty quickly last week. Did you have somewhere to be? Maybe...a date?"

"What? No. Like I said, I had that cupcake order."

He raised a brow, calling me on my bullshit.

"Brenna Simmons wanted twenty-four cupcakes for her sister's baby shower."

"Lame excuse I've seen you whip up a batch of cupcakes in half an hour."

I laughed. "No, she wanted dick cupcakes, as in, shaped like a dick."

"Come again?"

I snorted, and Ben laughed.

"How do you even...do you have to shape them? Like cake-pops?" Ben said, making dick shaping gestures with his hands and laughing harder.

"No, I have penis cupcake tins. That part of the job was easy. It was the part where I had to cover them in fondant and make them look realistic. *That* was the hard part. No pun intended. I even had to make spun sugar for the pubes."

By the time I finished we were both crying with laughter, and Ben's earlier interest was forgotten.

"Please tell me you took photos."

I nodded and got my phone out. I always took photos of my cakes for my website and social media pages, but this one was purely for entertainment value because there was no way I'd ever advertise that I'd spent a whole evening looking at dick pics on my laptop so I could make realistic cupcakes for Brenna Simmons.

A knock on the door made us both jump and laugh even harder.

Spilled Beans was closed on Sundays, which was why I'd asked Ben to come today because we could take our time.

I was about to send away whoever was at the door when I saw Tristan's face through the glass.

"Oh look, your fiancé is here. Let's see how much he really *does* love you when he finds out you had cake already."

"Nah, he promised, and his promises are golden."

Ben's innocent words settled like lead in the pit of my stomach. I'd once believed that. Golden promises that were never going to be broken because we loved each other so much.

I got up to unlock the door and shook my head as if it would easily shake away the direction of my thoughts and that feeling that always settled in me whenever I thought about the past. The past was better left there, my mom always said. Right...

"Hey, Tristan, hope you're hungry because..." My words

were stuck in my throat when Tate followed Tristan in. What was he doing here?

"Um...hi...Tate,"

He came right up to me, smelling all woodsy and citrusy, placed a kiss on my cheek, and whispered in my ear, "I've been thinking about your buns all week."

I coughed and pushed him away, giving him a stern look that said 'no funny business.'

"So, what goodies have you got for us? When Tristan said there was free cake, I just couldn't resist," he said, sitting at the table.

"You came all the way from Boston for free cake?"

"What can I say, when a guy has a taste of your buns, he has to wonder what else you're hiding in that mixing bowl."

I groaned, hoping the rapidly growing problem in my jeans wouldn't show through the Spilled Beans apron.

What was it with my body reacting to this guy? First of all, I didn't even know him. Second of all, he was Tristan's brother. And third of all—

"Indy?"

"Sorry, what?"

"The guys are dying to taste the cakes," Ben said.

"Oh yes, um... of course. Let me prepare an extra plate."

Despite my strange momentary lapse of concentration, when I looked at Ben grinning, I couldn't help smiling, too. He was getting his second helping of the cakes after all.

"The first two cakes from the left are Madeira cake with a buttercream filling," I explained. "That cake basically goes with everything. I've also given you strawberry and chocolate hazelnut. The third cake is a chocolate cake with a salted caramel buttercream filling, the fourth cake is lemon and lavender, and the last one is a cinnamon coffee cake with pecans. I also have a list of other flavors I can make for you if you want to try them. I picked these based on your favorite pastries and cakes."

I watched as Tristan, Tate, and Ben had a piece of each

cake and then gave me feedback on each of the flavors. They also loved my idea for the design of the cake, and I couldn't have been more delighted. Three tiers with one side decorated with books and the other with various home design items, such as rolls of fabric, paint cans, and furniture. The designs met in the front with both figurines of Tristan and Ben sitting on a table, with a bookshelf behind them.

"Honestly, guys, I'm going to love baking this cake so much," I said as they all got up to leave with a box of leftover cake.

"I'll catch up with you in a minute," Tate said. Tristan nodded and put his arm around Ben while they walked out toward Bookmarked.

The door closed behind them, and suddenly, I was very aware that even though the door was unlocked, this was the first time since that night at the motel that we'd been on our own.

I started clearing the trays as an excuse for something to do.

Tate looked around at the pictures I had on the walls of coffee beans from around the world, at the empty display cabinet, and then at me.

He came around the counter. Each step he moved toward me was a step I took back until I was trapped between him and the wall.

I should push him away, I should tell him to go, and I should definitely not be aware of every single fiber in my body and how they seemed to vibrate with Tate's closeness.

"How...how can I help you? Did you want more cake to take home? I may still have some left in the back," I said, hoping my voice sounded measured and controlled rather than breathy and desperate.

"Can I see you?" he asked. His gaze, so intense but with a little frown in between his eyebrows. It was as though he thought he knew what he wanted, but he wasn't sure why he wanted it.

And don't I know the feeling.

"Why?"

"I don't...please, Indy. Can I see you later?"

"I'm not sure if it's a good idea." In fact, I knew it was a terrible idea. The worst.

"I won't push you to...you know. I just want to spend time with you."

This was definitely a bad idea, but what the hell, if we were going to be best men together, we should at least be friends, right?

"Okay, sure. Meet me upstairs in my apartment, through the stairs on the side of the building."

He smiled and left.

Suddenly, the four walls of my coffee shop felt empty without Tate here.

I stared at him as he crossed the square until he walked inside Bookmarked.

Somewhere in the back of my mind were my mother's words about a change in the wind.

TATE

As I walked back to Bookmarked from Spilled Beans, I tried with zero success to wipe the big smile off my face because Indy had agreed to see me later.

I had to give myself a pat on the back for lasting a whole week without contacting him using the hookup app. But driving all the way back to Chester Falls only seven days after I was first there and without a reasonable excuse was a new level of obsession.

Tate Brooks didn't do obsession.

Tate Brooks didn't do thinking about a man past the cooling cum stage.

But I hadn't hooked up with Indy. I hadn't even kissed him. If anything, I'd be the last person he'd want to see after last week.

I'd nearly turned the car around back to Boston several times, but with each interchange, I passed and kept going, I was closer to Indy, closer to my brother, and there was something about the countryside that untied all the knots in my back. It was as if all the shit from the past week had been shoved into a box and left behind.

I hadn't even thought of an excuse to see Indy, but then

I'd arrived and found out Tristan was on his way to Spilled Beans to meet Ben for their cake testing.

It was as if life was once again giving me lemons, even though most of the time I either didn't know what to do with them or I'd let them go rotten.

As soon as I'd seen Indy looking so shocked to see me but so stunningly beautiful with his defined jaw, full lips, and hair tied up in a bun, I'd be damned if I wasn't craving a sip of lemonade.

Indy responded to my presence as if I was a radio frequency that only he could tune into, and I couldn't help wonder what would happen if we let ourselves listen to the music?

The only way to find the answer was to spend time with him, but first I needed to make my presence in Chester Falls plausible by spending some time with my brother and his fiancé.

I heard the excited chattering even before I reached the door to Bookmarked, which had been left unlocked for me.

When I got up to the apartment, I was surprised to see a small guy on his knees in front of Ben and a bigger guy sitting on the sofa smirking and shaking his head.

"What's going on?" I asked.

The guy on his knees poked his head from around Ben and gasped when he saw me.

"Oh. My. Coco. It *is* true," he gasped.

"Huh?"

Tristan introduced them as Tom, the owner of the fashion store next door, and Wren, his boyfriend.

Of course. They must be having their measurements taken for the wedding suits.

Tristan had confirmed earlier this week that they'd found an officiant available to marry them in September, but this was April. Wasn't it too early to be thinking about suits?

My stomach started churning, probably because of all the cake.

"Um, nice to meet you guys. I didn't realize you were busy this afternoon. I'll make my way home," I said.

"You're not going anywhere, Sunshine. At least not until I've had my way with you. Don't worry, I'll be gentle. You won't feel a thing."

"Tom," the other guy, Wren, warned.

Tom shrugged his shoulders and went back to what he was doing, which now that I'd seen a measuring tape on his hand and a small notebook on the floor, made total sense.

"Do you already have someone to make your suit?" Ben asked.

"Um no." *Because normal people don't get a suit for a wedding six months before the event.*

"Tom is the best. I mean, I've never had one of his suits, but I love his bespoke shirts. They're so comfortable to wear."

Tom looked between Tristan and me.

"You are so alike and yet...not," he said.

Tristan chuckled. "We've heard that once or...a million times, haven't we, old man?"

"Apples and oranges. Chalk and cheese. That's us, kiddo."

"Hey, Hot Cakes, I'm making Tight Buns his suit, too, so I can get you to match. I'll even give you a discount. Hell, just measuring you up will be worth my time alone," Tom said.

Had he just called me...and Indy...?

"He really doesn't mean that," Wren said. "What he means is that he'll be happy to take your measurements in a professional manner and will charge you the appropriate amount of money for the suit."

Tom huffed and stood up to measure Ben's sleeve length.

"Sounds like you just clarified his words with the fine print. Mitigating potential lawsuits?" I said to Wren. "Must be a full-time job." I chuckled.

"It is," Wren said, "but it's the best job I've ever had. I even get paid in cupcakes."

"With thick frosting and extra sprinkles," Tom finished.

"What he means is—"

I raised my hand. "I got it, no need to explain it further."

"So," Tristan said, "how do you feel about a new suit?"

I considered it for a moment. I'd noticed the window display next door, and if Tom had designed those clothes, he was pretty good.

Damnit, I'd fallen prey to their fun banter, but I didn't want a suit, and I didn't want to think about my brother's wedding. Not yet, at least.

The room was getting really hot. Was Chester Falls getting an early summer?

"Oh shit, I'm so sorry, but I need to go. I just remembered I have to prepare for a meeting tomorrow and still have to face the city traffic."

Tristan raised a brow but didn't say anything.

It wasn't until I was outside that I took a full deep breath and then walked across the square again to see Indy.

Most buildings in the square looked the same but it was interesting that while access to Ben's apartment was through the store, Indy had a separate entrance on his side of the building.

I ran my hands over my face, scratching my beard and smoothing it back before I rang the bell. I didn't even know what I was doing wanting to see Indy.

"Hey, come in," he said, opening the door.

With every step I took inside Indy's apartment, my heart rate increased by a few beats.

"I'm sorry about last week. I shouldn't have said those things and implied that we could... you know..."

I let my words hang. Indy was still by the door, his face indecipherable.

"Why did you?" he said, taking a step closer.

"Because I'm a jackass. Because I couldn't stop thinking about the guy I saw walking into the bar while I was waiting for T1ghtBuns."

He took another step closer. I still couldn't read him, but he wasn't running away or throwing me out, which I took for a good thing.

"What did you think of that guy?"

I smiled as Indy took another step toward me, putting him within reaching distance. I tucked a loose strand of indigo hair behind his ear.

"Confident, cool, self-assured. I saw someone who knows who they are and has embraced it. I admire that."

He smiled, but it didn't reach his eyes.

"Sometimes things aren't as they seem," he said.

"I know, Indy...I know."

I felt as if there was something lodged in my throat.

"I'm sorry you didn't get to meet that Indy." His words were a whisper.

"I'm not. That guy still lives inside you, even when he's doing his best to resist unwanted advances."

We were so close that the little hairs on my arms stood up. The electrical current between us could power a small village, and I was almost afraid of what would happen if we took a step back, and even more scared of what would happen if we closed the distance.

"They weren't, Tate. They weren't."

His dark blue eyes bore into mine looking for something. Clues? Answers?

"Weren't what?"

"Unwanted," he breathed out.

Whatever was happening outside, inside Indy's apartment, time had slowed down. Like in those David Attenborough nature documentaries when they show a hummingbird drinking nectar from a flower and then slow it down to the point we can see the detail of their wing feathers.

Just like the hummingbird looked like they were hovering, thanks to their super fast movement of the wings, so did Indy and I.

Hearts beating at over one thousand beats per minute, hovering just above the point of no return.

"Tate," Indy pleaded. We were so close I felt his breath on my beard.

My hand had been resting on his neck since I'd tucked his hair out of the way. One tiny hummingbird size move was all it took to tilt his face up.

Indy's hands rested on my waist, his fingers slowly fisting the fabric of my shirt until I felt it tight against my skin.

We hadn't yet kissed, and I was almost afraid to do it because I didn't want this moment to end. This perfect moment where decisions hadn't been made, consequences hadn't been found.

Except I was wrong. Perfection was when Indy's lips met mine. It was so slow I felt the slight tremble of his lips as they pressed together to pull gently on mine. And then again, and again.

I thought I heard thunder outside. Maybe rain. The world could end for all I cared.

There wasn't a single demand made. No deepening of the kiss. All hands were in safe places.

It was at the same time the tamest and the hottest kiss of my entire life.

Now I knew what it felt like to be a hummingbird.

David Attenborough had a lot to answer for.

INDY

*W*hen I was fourteen, my mom told me about the butterfly effect. At the time she was teaching me a lesson. *"Don't overlook what people tell you, however inconsequential it may seem. Listen, Indy, and you may learn the most important lessons,"* she'd said.

I'd become obsessed with it, and, being my mother's son and a born hopeless romantic, I'd dreamed of the day I'd be kissed so gently but so perfectly that I'd start a storm outside.

The logical part of me, the same part of me that measured ingredients meticulously, knew it was an impossibility.

It still didn't stop me from wishing for that kiss or paying attention to all the things around me whenever I kissed someone. You know, just in case.

When I'd been with the supposed love of my life, there had been no effects, no storms. Then again, those kisses had never been gentle. They'd been rushed, frantic as if we were on borrowed time.

Not now. The moment Tate tilted my head up and his lips touched mine, the clock on the wall stopped. Everything intensified. His beard was softer than I'd expected, and every brush of his lips was as if he was kissing all those spots on my body that no one had touched in a long time, maybe ever.

And it was raining. No, not raining, storming.

I needed to stop this kiss. All the red lights were going off in my head, but just like no one can drive past a car crash and not look, I was unable to pull away from Tate.

How could I? With his hands cradling my face, his soft thumbs running up and down my cheek, I'd never felt so much like I was floating and grounded all at the same time.

In the same way it started, the kiss ended. One more soft kiss and Tate pulled back.

I opened my eyes slowly, afraid of what I'd see.

Tate still had his eyes closed, but his hands hadn't left my face or stopped the motion with his thumbs.

"Tate..." I whispered.

He leaned his forehead against mine.

"Oh, Indy... What do we do now?" he said, letting out a breath.

I had no clue what to say. Before the kiss, I could make up all the assumptions about Tate in my head. Anything I could come up with to keep my distance was fair game.

Now? My brain was Confusion Central, and all the trains were arriving at the same time.

"Movie?" I said.

He pulled away and looked into my eyes.

"That...sounds great, actually."

I released his shirt, stealing a quick glance at his hard chest, and took a deep breath.

"What do you want to watch? I have Netflix or some good old fashioned DVDs," I said.

"You have DVDs? I can't remember the last time I saw one."

"I like how they make me feel when I watch them."

I went to the kitchen to put some popcorn on the stovetop. Tate was quiet, so I poked my head through the open archway and saw him looking at me.

"How do they make you feel?" he asked.

"I don't know how to explain. The picture then didn't have the high definition it does now, but I like it. It makes it feel more...real. Like the story is more important. I'm not sure I'm making any sense."

"It makes sense." He smiled and started looking through the DVDs.

If Tate was a date or a hookup, I'd have hidden my collection. No one needed to know my obsession with romantic movies.

Tate was none of those things, so even though I wanted to tell him to forget it and watch whatever was new on Netflix, I forced myself to stay still and watch as he ran his finger over the titles on the shelf by the TV.

"So I guess sci-fi or thrillers are out," he said.

"Um, yeah...I kinda have an obsession, as you can see. We can watch Netflix if you want."

"No," he said, shaking his head. "Let's watch a romantic movie. Grab the tissues and the nail polish. Oh, and that popcorn better have a ton of sugar."

I went back to the kitchen, biting my lip to hide my smile, and opened the cupboard to get the vanilla sugar for the popcorn.

When I went back to the living room, Tate was sitting on the sofa with a small pile of DVDs on his lap. I put the bowl of popcorn on the coffee table and sat next to it.

"What are the options?" I asked.

"*Four Weddings and a Funeral, Wedding Date, My Best Friend's Wedding, Runaway Bride, My Big Fat Greek Wedding, Made of Honor,* or *The Wedding Planner.*"

"I see we have a theme..." I said.

"To be fair, most of these movies have weddings. Which one's your favorite?"

"I don't have one," I said.

Tate quirked a brow. "Okay, let's pretend for a second I believe you, so we're going to start by removing the weakest candidates."

"*Four Weddings and A Funeral* can go," I said.

"Agreed. Can't stand Hugh Grant's floppiness."

I chuckled.

"What's next?" he asked. *"Wedding Planner?"*

We both said 'alright, alright, alright' out loud, and then started laughing.

"How about we watch *Made of Honor*?" I suggested.

He pulled a face. "Too close to home."

"Why did you pick it?"

"Patrick Dempsey. And it seemed like a good idea."

"Like kissing me?"

Tate dropped the DVDs on the sofa and pulled me by the hand so I had no choice but to straddle him.

Mayday! Mayday!

This was not the best position for us to be in considering how all of the time I was near Tate, I was sporting wood.

"Indy," he said, running his hands up and down my arms before resting them on my legs. "I would never regret anything with you. Maybe some things could be a bad idea, but it doesn't mean I'd regret them," he said.

"I'm sorry. I don't know why I said that. My mouth decided to speak without asking permission."

"How interesting..." he said, tilting his head. One corner of his mouth raised up into a half-smile.

"What is?"

"If your delicious mouth tends to speak for itself, I think I'll want to spend more time with you, and see what your mouth has to say."

"It's a good thing you have an excuse then," I said.

"What's that?"

"The wedding."

He nodded, but his smile left him. Somehow, despite our kiss, despite acknowledging that we were both into each other, I didn't feel like I could ask him about it.

"This is taking too long. We're watching *The Wedding Date*, because Dermot Mulroney, and I'm going to need far more sugar then I see on that popcorn," he said before he kissed my nose and moved me to sit next to him on the sofa.

He got up and walked to the kitchen. My brain didn't engage in time to instruct my mouth to say something.

"Indy?"

"Hmmm?"

"Why does your kitchen look like the Pornhub version of *Baking with Martha Stewart*?"

I groaned and hid my face in my hands.

I hate my family.

"I so want to play the guessing game, but my gut tells me the real story is a lot more fun to hear." He said, sitting next to me.

"Can't we just put the film on?"

"Nope."

He picked up the bowl, sprinkling a generous amount of sugar and cinnamon, and turned to face me, grabbing a handful of popcorn and stuffing it in his mouth.

"You're a savage."

He winked and licked his lips in a way that was one hundred percent intended to reach my dick.

"Fine. I was nervous about coming out to my parents. Not because they were homophobic or anything, but because our family is very close. They always talked about grandchildren as if it was a given."

"Gay men can have kids, too," he said.

"I know, but I was thirteen. Kids were so far off in the future, and I wanted to make my parents happy."

"Okay, so what does that have to do with the excessive amount of dick in your kitchen?"

"I worked myself into such a state that I muddled all my words, and in the middle of my carefully thought through speech, I blurted that I like cock."

"You...said you like cock...to your parents..." Tate said slowly, clearly trying to stop his laughter from bursting out.

"My brother, too." I took the bowl from Tate and grabbed some of the popcorn. "Jesus, how much sugar does this have?"

"It's still not as sweet as you, but..." he said, motioning for me to finish the story.

"Ugh, I hate you. After my little speech, nothing happened. My parents were fine with me being gay. A few weeks later, I received a package in the mail. It was a blanket with tiny dicks on it. Then it was underwear, then a dick shaped plate and cutlery. It was funny, but I thought it would stop when I moved out."

"Did it?"

I pointed to the kitchen. "You walked into exhibit A and the reason I rarely bring anyone here. After I moved, I made the mistake of giving them a key for emergencies. Apparently, for my family, needing cock-shaped bakeware, wall clock, or hanging decorations constitutes an emergency."

"You could take them down," he suggested.

"They do this when I'm not here. I've learned to embrace the crazy."

"Wow."

The rain seemed to ease off outside.

"Do you still want to watch the movie? I know you have a long drive."

"Yes, if you still want to..."

Tate's words carried an element of uncertainty, so I grabbed the DVD and set everything up before sitting back on the couch next to him.

As the opening credits rolled on, he put his arm around my shoulders and pulled me closer.

Leaning on his bigger body and feeling the motion of his

breathing lulled me to sleep even before the movie was halfway through.

I felt a hand gently running through my long hair as I found my way back to consciousness.

"Your hair is so soft," he said.

"Did it come loose?"

"You seemed uncomfortable, so I pulled your hairband off. I hope it's okay."

I sat up straighter and tied my hair back up.

"Yeah, it felt nice," I smiled.

"Indy?"

"Yeah?"

He stared into my eyes, his lighter blue ones looked tired.

"Can I...could I stay over tonight?

TATE

" $\mathcal{E}$ arth to Tate."

"What? Sorry, I was somewhere else. What did you say?"

When my best friend Harrison invited me for some grilled steaks at his place, I figured it was a good idea. I mean, we're talking steak, beer, and good company.

The problem was that it had been a week since I'd seen Indy, and if I stopped bullshitting myself, I'd admit that the reason I'd accepted Harrison's invitation was so I wouldn't drive unannounced to Chester Falls, again.

"Stella is dropping Megan off in an hour, so unless you want to watch Trolls again, I'd run for it. You've been warned."

I laughed. "Nah, I'll stay. Haven't seen my favorite goddaughter in a while. She must miss me."

"Oh yeah, you're a fucking ray of sunshine."

"Screw you," I said, unscrewing a beer and throwing the cap at him.

"Never again, you're too toppy."

I laughed. "What's that supposed to mean?"

"Nevermind. What I want to know is what has you so distracted."

"I'm salivating for some more of your amazing steak. That's why I can't think straight," I said, giving him my biggest 'feed me' grin.

"I'll give you steak with one condition."

I raised a brow and took a sip from my beer.

"Who's the guy? You promised I could live vicariously through you, and I can't do that without details."

"You know you could still get out there and meet someone, right? Why don't you?"

"Because I'm not ready. You know how much it hurt when Stella left me. How much it still hurts that I don't get to put my daughter to bed every day."

"I know, Hare, but you're not dead. You're in your mid-thirties. Your dick could fall off."

He laughed.

"Dramatic much? Now talk or those steaks will never see the grill, let alone touch it."

"I'm going to grab the steaks from the fridge to make sure you don't break your promise," I said, heading toward the double doors from the back porch to the kitchen.

My phone buzzed with a text, and my stomach flipped a little when I saw Indy's name on the screen.

I still couldn't believe I'd spent another full night with Indy and all that had happened was that I was still very much sexually frustrated and annoyed with myself at my newly found restraint around him. But... I'd convinced him to give me his number, so there was that.

Indy: Breaking News: Tom is in charge of planning the honeymoon.

Tate: I've only met him for a total of ten minutes, but I feel that decision is Ben and Tristan compromising.

Indy: He wanted to be the wedding planner.

Tate: Dear lord.

Indy: He'd be awesome at it, but I think Ben and Tristan want a slightly more low key wedding event than what Tom had in mind.

Tate: He sounds like my worst nightmare.

Indy: You're saying you wouldn't want an ice sculpture of you and your future husband greeting your guests as they come in?

Tate: I'm saying I'll never get married, so I'm glad I'll never need to make a decision on that particular topic.

"Hey, you're grabbing the steaks or making love to them?" Harrison shouted from the porch.

"Hold on, I'm coming."

"That's what he said."

The text bubbles on the screen kept moving and then disappearing, so I put the phone back in my pocket and went back outside.

"How's the Davenport case going," Harrison asked, placing the steaks on the grill.

"Fuck, it's pushing all my buttons. The husband is a douche."

"Most of the time they are, and we know this, which is why we're good at our jobs. Whether or not we agree with it, we know our clients. What's different about this one that's getting to you?"

I huffed and started clearing up the plates and empty bottles from earlier.

"He's too much like him."

"Your old man?"

"Yeah."

Harrison was the only person I'd ever trusted with my personal stuff. Even Tristan didn't know what had happened after our parents divorced and we were divided as if we were a box of trinkets instead of children.

My phone buzzed in my pocket again, and I went for it without thinking.

Indy: *Dirty Dancing* is on later.
Tate: No one puts Baby in a corner.
Indy: Oh my god, you are a secret romance movie watcher.
Tate: No comment on advice of my lawyer.
Indy: Your lawyer sucks.
Tate: Like you wouldn't believe.
Indy: Tate!

I smiled at the thought of Indy's dark blue eyes open wide as he told me off.

"Hold on to the guy, Tate," Harrison said.

I passed him clean plates for the steaks.

"There's no guy, Hare."

"Then I want to know what's in your phone that put that smooshy look on your face."

Whenever I had good news, Harrison was the first one to hear it. If I had a shit day, I could knock on his office door and grab a couple of beers after work.

He was more than a friend, but there was something we fundamentally disagreed on. Marriage and relationships.

"I nearly hooked up with my brother's fiancé's best man," I confessed.

"Wait, let me grab a beer because this has to be good," he said, adding some salad to his plate and picking a beer from the cool box.

"You're an ass, you know that, right?"

"Yup." He nodded.

I gave him the short version, skipping the part where I'd spent a total of four hours staring at Indy's sleeping face, the part where I'd been researching the best romance movies of all time, and especially skipping the part where we kissed.

"So you propositioned the guy, he said no, you propositioned him again, and now you're friends?"

I laughed. "What can I say? Contrary to popular belief, I'm actually quite charming."

He raised an eyebrow. Sadly, I didn't have anything to throw at him, and the steak was too good to waste.

I was saved from taking the conversation further by the bell announcing Megan's arrival.

"Uncle Tate!" she shouted, running toward me. I picked her up and lifted her up in the air.

"Well hello, Ladybug. Where did you learn to fly so high?"

She rolled her eyes at me and said, "I can't fly, Uncle Tate. I'm not a *real* ladybug."

"Of course. Ladybugs prefer to lay on the flowers. Is that why you smell so nice?" I lifted her again, pretending to smell her, and placed a raspberry in her tummy. She giggled until I stopped and lowered her down to my hip.

"Uncle Tate, can we watch Trolls?"

"I see I'm no longer the master of this household," Harrison said, holding a small pink backpack. "Honey, can you go put your bag in your bedroom? We'll watch Trolls after, okay?"

"Okay, Daddy. You can put me down now, Uncle Tate."

I kissed her on the cheek and watched as she ran toward her room.

"Everything okay with Stella?" I asked.

"Yeah, same old."

I hated to see my friend hurting, especially when the only thing I could do to help was the one thing he'd totally vetoed because he didn't want to risk taking Stella to court and losing access to Megan.

Despite her excitement and the unlimited energy only a five-year-old had, Megan fell asleep halfway through Trolls, so I made my way home.

Harrison lived less than a mile from me, so I always walked when I knew I'd be drinking. The days were getting warmer now, but the nights were still chilly, so I must have turned a different way in a bid to get home faster because I walked past a small bakery I hadn't seen before.

The window display was full of cupcakes of all kinds. I hadn't been to Spilled Beans while it was open and wondered if Indy's cupcake displays were as colorful.

The bakery was still open, so I went in. It smelled delicious inside, so after taking my time picking a cupcake, I ended up with a box with two cupcakes and two cinnamon buns.

I ate two of them before I got home.

Tate: I cheated on you, and it wasn't worth it. I'm so sorry.
Indy: My heart will start bleeding as soon as you provide some detail of said cheating.
Tate: I found a new bakery near me.
Indy: *Gasps* You didn't.
Tate: I did, but it wasn't worth it. Your buns are eighty percent more delicious.
Indy: Eighty? I need to up my game. How can I earn those twenty percent?
Tate: I'll tell you one day.
Tate: Can I watch *Dirty Dancing* with you?

The speech bubbles appeared and then disappeared.

I went to my room to change into a t-shirt and sweatpants while I waited for Indy's reply.

Five minutes later, I was on my couch, ready for my second movie of the evening. The pile of paperwork I'd promised myself to work on after seeing Harrison was forgotten on the kitchen table.

My phone rang, and I saw Indy's name on the display.

"Hey, did you mean to ring, or was it a butt-dial?" I asked. "Not gonna lie, I'd be super happy if you told me your butt dialed me."

He laughed, and I imagined him sitting on his couch with his hair down and legs crossed.

"It wasn't a butt dial."

"You mean...you actually wanted to speak to me? Look how far we've come."

"Ass."

He went quiet, so I looked at the phone to see if it had been disconnected, but the call was still on.

"Tate?"

"Yes?"

"When are you...um...coming back to Chester Falls?"

"In a couple of weeks. Tristan gave Tom my number, and he wouldn't stop texting me until I agreed to go there so he can measure me for the suit."

"Okay."

"Was there anything you wanted to ask me?"

"Um, no. Do you still want to watch the film together?"

I smiled to myself and changed the call to a video call. He answered after a few rings.

"That's better," I said, smiling at him. He looked tired. It was only nine in the evening, but I guessed Indy must have been up early. "How about we watch the film together until you fall asleep?"

"That would be perfect."

"Place the phone on that table you have next to your couch. I want to see you."

The image was wobbly for a moment until he got his phone in place, and I did the same.

If anyone quizzed me about the movie, I wouldn't have been able to answer any questions because Indy fell asleep within five minutes of the film starting, and I spent the next hour and a half watching him.

My only regret was that I wasn't there to take him to bed. Sex was the furthest thing on my mind, which should have raised big alarm bells in my head to stay away from Indy.

INDY

$\mathcal{M}$ost days I was thankful for the morning rush. The look in my customer's eyes whenever I filled the trays with fresh cupcakes or pastries was priceless, and the scent of fresh coffee that never left Spilled Beans was like my own energy source.

Today, however, it seemed that the morning rush was never going to end and every customer was extra picky.

"Why are you so fidgety today?" Jake asked. "You're moving like you've had a sip from every cup of coffee you've served."

"I'm not fidgety. The line isn't going down today, and I don't want to leave you on your own to deal with it."

"It's only ten o'clock, Indy. The line *isn't* meant to go down yet."

The clock on the wall, unfortunately, agreed with Jake. Traitor.

"Calm down, boss. We want the business, otherwise how can you afford that pay rise you promised me?"

I gave my customer the change for his order and looked at Jake, who was grinning back at me.

"Morning, Indy."

"Morning, Maggie, what can I get you?"

She looked around and then said with a shy smile, "A chai latte, and, um...a large black coffee."

I thought my eyes were going to bulge out their sockets.

"Does that mean..." I said.

She nodded, her light skin turning a pretty shade of pink.

I made her order and put two pastries for her in a bag.

"This one's on the house for the brave hearts."

"Thank you, Indy."

Maggie left with a big smile on her face and a spring in her step. I'd bet my bottom dollar she was headed to Slade's vintage bike shop where Liam worked.

"You should change the name of this place from Spilled Beans to Cupid's Arrow," Jake said.

We worked through the line together, and it wasn't until after eleven that I had a chance to get back to the kitchen to tidy up and start on preparations for tomorrow's bakes.

I'd left my phone next to the stand mixer, so I saw when the screen lit up with a message.

Tate: Every single person that left Spilled Beans this morning had a big smile on their face. What kind of magic powers do you have?

I looked up instinctively as if I could see across the square, which I couldn't because I was in the kitchen.

Was Tate in Chester Falls already? I thought he wasn't arriving for a few hours.

I grabbed the phone and unlocked the screen to reply, but before I had a chance, another message popped up.

Tate: Are there any side effects to your magic? Because my sweet tooth is craving a bite of your buns.

Indy: Why don't you come over and see for yourself?

Tate: Why don't you come out of the kitchen and serve your favorite customer?

I nearly tripped on the broom I had leaning against the kitchen counter on my way to the front.

Smooth, Indy. Smooth. Now take a deep breath and go out there like you haven't been daydreaming about the gorgeous, muscly, tree man with the sexy beard.

When I came out, I was met with another long line of customers, a flustered Jake, and Tate sitting by the window sipping on a coffee like he belonged there.

"Fuck, Jake, why didn't you call me?" I whispered.

"I did."

"I'm sorry. I must have been distracted."

He looked at me with a raised brow.

"Shut up," I said.

Every time we served a customer, another two came in. The pace didn't let up until almost lunchtime. Fortunately, it was Friday, so the part-time girl I'd recently hired to work would be here any moment to help Jake out.

And then the best part of my day would start, and not only because Tate was here and had been looking at me like he wanted to lick me head to toe. No, because that wouldn't happen. We were just friends, and we had wedding stuff to do together.

I hung my apron behind the kitchen door and picked up the keys to my car before going back out.

"Keep him away for the rest of the day, please. I'd like to close on time, and I have no clue how to handle the lovey-dovey shit," Jake said to Tate, who was leaning against the counter with a new cup of coffee in hand.

"I'm going to pretend I didn't hear that," I said to Jake and then turned to Tate, "and you, drink up. My car is a no-food, no-drink, no-mess zone."

"Ohhh, you must be special," Jake said to Tate.

"Why's that?" Tate asked.

I ignored Jake's teasing and walked out of Spilled Beans and into the sunny square. It was the perfect day.

"What was he talking about?" Tate said, catching up with me as I turned to a side street where my special car lived in the garage I rented out.

"You'll see."

I pressed the button to open the garage door, the heady rush I had every time I drove this car already coursing through my veins.

"Indy..."

"Yes?" I said in my most nonchalant voice.

Tate looked at me and then at the shiny red paint of the car. He walked all the way around before meeting me by the driver's door.

"You have a 1965 convertible Ford Mustang," he said, almost a little breathless. Yup, I knew the feeling.

"Yes."

Tate smiled and shook his head.

"I keep on trying to find reasons to keep away from you, but every single time we meet, you surprise me, Indy."

He came closer, trapping me against the car, a position I seemed to find myself in with Tate more often than not. His breath smelled of coffee and cinnamon, and along with his woodsy aftershave, were both making my head spin and my cock harden. Why did I have to be so fucking attracted to this man?

"Wow, I'm a bike man, but fuck, she's beautiful."

Tate jumped away from me like he'd been burned. I breathed out, relieved for the interruption.

"Hey, Slade, what's up?" I said.

He raised his coffee cup. "Maggie came by to see Liam, so I thought I'd give myself a break and leave them to chat."

"Glad you could get away. This is Tate, by the way. He's Tristan's brother."

Slade nodded. "Nice to meet you. I thought you looked familiar. If you're ever on the market for a good bike, just drop by. I reckon you're a Harley man, am I right? My shop is just around the corner from Spilled Beans."

"I'm not into bikes, but thanks," Tate replied.

I turned to Tate, but his eyes were fixed on Slade. I couldn't blame him, since Slade, with his salt and pepper hair, and light blue eyes was every bit the sexy silver fox.

"Anyway," I said. "I'm so happy Liam gave Maggie a chance. He needs someone like her in his life."

"Don't we all," Slade said, taking a sip from his to-go cup. "I best get going. Come by the shop some time. I'd love to know more about your car. It's a classic."

I nodded and watched as Slade left.

"What was that?" I asked Tate.

"What was what?"

I sighed. "Nevermind. Are you ready to go?"

"Are your buns the yummiest ever?"

I chuckled. "Come on, get in the car, and *don't* make a mess."

He tilted his head and winked at me before going around the car to the passenger door. "I think I like this bossy Indy."

I groaned. This man was going to be the death of me.

Tell me, god, why am I not jumping him? Ugh.

I'd already pulled the top back yesterday when I'd checked the weather and saw it was going to be a warm, sunny day, so we were ready to drive off.

As soon as we were on the highway, I put my foot on the gas.

With the sun on my face, the wind blowing around me, and the roar of the car engine, I felt like anything was possible.

I looked at Tate, who was grinning back at me. He stretched his arms over his shoulders and put his hands behind his head, looking forward.

We still had a few miles to go and couldn't hear each other

over the noise of the car and the wind, so I put my foot down further and enjoyed the ride until we had to turn off the highway.

This was the life. Freedom. A great car. A gorgeous man next to me, and somewhere to go.

I could ignore the little voices in my head that were telling me to be careful. Over the noise of the car, they were barely audible. Maybe just for the next few miles, I could pretend this was my life.

Such an easy thing to do when I looked again at Tate and saw all the things I wanted to see. Wonder. Affection. Lust.

TATE

$\mathcal{I}$'d never seen anyone looking so free, so relaxed, and so at ease as Indy did driving his Mustang, considering I was pretty sure he was breaking some speeding laws, too.

It didn't matter. I'd argue with any officer that dared to break the happy spell he was under.

Fortunately, we had a smooth ride all the way to our destination, wherever that was. I just hoped Indy had forgotten my little moment of jealousy earlier, or at least that he hadn't read it as that.

I'd wanted to thank Slade for interrupting what would have inevitably been a kiss, but watching the familiarity between Indy and the silver-haired man was enough to shake me up.

As we wound back up on country roads, my attention went back to Indy. His bun had mostly come undone, leaving loose tendrils of his blue hair flying around his face.

There was a happy smile on his face, which didn't fade when he looked at me.

We drove through an open gate with a wooden plaque on the side that said Knox Farm.

The place had a long driveway with tall trimmed hedges on either side, so it was impossible to know what was beyond it or what kind of farm this was.

After a while, I saw a large circular building come into view. There were quite a few cars in the parking lot but I didn't see anyone around.

It wasn't until we were stopped that I felt it.

"What's that smell?"

Indy smiled as he rearranged his hair and said, "It's lavender. Delicious, isn't it?"

"It's nice. I like it."

"This is a lavender farm. Come on, let's go in."

I helped him get the top of the car up since he didn't want the pollen and dust to get inside.

"This place is amazing. I need to see the owner to get my order, but then I'm going to show you the best place on earth."

I nodded and placed my hand on Indy's lower back as we walked inside the building. If I didn't know any better, I'd say he leaned back on me a little.

"Indy!"

A guy about the same height as me but about a fifty pounds lighter approached us.

"Hey, Reed," Indy said, greeting him. "This is Tate. Tate, this is Reed Knox. He owns the farm."

"Nice to meet you, Tate."

I shook his hand and followed as he gestured for us to go through a door to the side into what looked like an office.

From the outside, the building looked like a giant chalet like the ones you'd see up in the Rockies. From the inside, despite all the wooden walls, everything was modern.

All around Reed's office there were photographs of purple flowers, which I guessed were lavender.

"I bet you're thinking what's a farmer doing with such a high tech office, right?" Reed said.

I raised my hands and smiled. "No judging here. If you

have to spend hours in it, make it the best. Can't tell you how many times I've slept the night in my office. My back appreciates the expensive sofa I got."

"If my Pops was alive, he'd be telling me to get out and get my hands dirty, get stung by a couple of bees, and not come back until the sun was setting."

I liked Reed. He talked with his whole body like it was an extension of his words.

"Righty-o, Indy, my man, I have something for you to try. Want a bite, too, Tate?"

"As long as it doesn't put me to sleep or make me fail the drug test at work, I'm game."

Reed shook his head and went over to a mini kitchen he had in one corner of the office, pulling out a box with crackers and a jar with a light yellow substance inside.

"Oh my god, is that..." Indy said, walking over to Reed.

"It is," Reed said. "This is, in my humble opinion, the best lavender honey you can find this side of the Atlantic."

He dipped a wooden utensil in the honey, twisted it, and let it drip onto two crackers. Then he gave them to us to try out.

The last time I'd seen Indy this excited was when we'd watched *Sweet Home, Alabama,* but then he was trying to cover up how much he loved the movie. Now there was nothing but sheer delight, and he hadn't even tasted the honey.

I waited for Indy to have his cracker first because I didn't want to miss his reaction.

Reed, bless him, had his eyes wide open in expectation while we both watched as Indy licked the cracker to taste the honey on its own, and then stuffed the cracker in his mouth.

"You've done it, Reed!"

Indy hugged Reed who looked like he'd shed the heaviest weight from his shoulders.

I tried my cracker. Indy's reaction hadn't been an exaggeration. The honey was delicious and it carried a hint of lavender that went perfectly with the cracker.

"This is good. Did you make it here, Reed?" I asked.

"Oh yes. This honey is the hardest to make," Reed said, holding up the jar to show the pure color in the light. "You see, our bees have only pollinated the lavender flowers so the flavor comes through in the honey. It's nearly impossible to get monofloral honey because the bees can pollinate any other flowers around the fields, but our hives seem to love the lavender, so I'm hoping we can get enough honey to sell with the right label."

"Monofloral honey is more expensive," Indy explained. "A few years ago, the farm was hit by a hail storm that destroyed the crops. Reed has been working hard to get the farm back on its feet."

My job was predictable. There was very little that could affect my income. I couldn't imagine what it'd be like to live dependent on the elements. Nature could give you beautiful delicious honey or destructive hail.

"I went to a wedding once and the bride and groom gave us these tiny presents..." I said, trying to think of the name for the little hand made soaps.

"Favors," Indy said.

"Yes, that's it. Could this be something Ben and Tristan would like for their wedding?"

Indy looked at me with a strange expression.

"What, is it not a good idea? I don't know anything about these things, but I got useless soap once, and I'd probably have enjoyed a tiny pot of honey. I'd totally have that with my breakfast the day after the wedding."

That little crease that I'd seen appear between Indy's eyes when he was asleep came back. I didn't know what it meant.

"Indy?"

"Um, yeah, that's a great idea, actually," he said.

"Perfect. Reed, would you be able to make them into tiny pots and get a special label for them or something?" I asked.

"Yes, of course."

"And make sure they have your logo and contact details. Maybe some guests will want to come to visit the farm," I added.

A quick call to Tristan and we were all set. They loved it and accepted it as my wedding gift, which ticked a big box for me since I had no idea what to give them.

Between that and loading Indy's car with the supplies he needed for Spilled Beans, I'd learned more about the various uses of lavender than I ever imagined.

Reed was a chatterbox when it came to talking about his business, but I didn't miss how much quieter he became when his farm manager came over with Indy's stuff.

Before they left us, Reed thanked me for the wedding favors order by giving me a small gift bag with edible samples of the stuff they sold in the farm store.

I leaned against the car and put my hands in my pockets. "I believe I was promised a visit to, and I quote, the best place on earth, unquote."

"I wouldn't want to break a promise."

"Would these be suitable pickings for the best place on earth?" I said, raising the gift bag.

Indy's smile threatened to outshine the sun. "They're perfect."

I followed him to a path leading to the back of the main building. We ended up in an orchard that was surrounded by a brick wall with a gate at the end.

Even if I'd been told what I was going to see, I'd still never imagine it to be like this. The gate opened up to a field of row upon row of lavender shrubs as far as I could see.

I couldn't speak because there was nothing I could say that did it justice.

"Close your eyes," Indy said.

He stopped and held my hand. We hadn't even walked very much further past the gate.

I did as he said.

"Breathe in."

The scent was subtle and strong all at the same time. It came and went with the breeze.

"Listen."

Holy hell, what was that? There was a hum in the breeze. Were there bees? Jesus, it sounded like a swarm.

I opened my eyes, and Indy chuckled.

"They're right in the middle of the field, so we can't see them. It's beautiful, right?"

I stared into his eyes, shining like marbles. His hair a little more blue under the sun. His hand warm in mine.

"Stunning."

INDY

With Tate looking at me like that, it was becoming harder and harder to remember why we shouldn't get involved.

It was one thing to kiss, even if it had been the single best kiss of anyone's lifetime. I'd argue that all the way to my grave. Never in the history of kisses had a kiss ever been as perfect as that.

It was another thing altogether, to do more than kiss. Even if my body had a way of gravitating toward Tate in the same way Reed's bees gravitated toward the lavender.

Tate's hand came up to tuck a strand of hair behind my ear. He seemed to do that a lot.

Maybe one more kiss wouldn't hurt, would it?

As if he could hear my thoughts, Tate narrowed the distance between us and pressed his lips against mine. His beard tickled my skin, making me wonder if he needed a trim, and his soft lips pulled on mine, encouraging me to have a taste of his.

The scent of lavender swirled around us, and the distant hum of the bees was our personal soundtrack.

Right at that moment, lavender and sweet honey became

my new favorite flavor. Strong arms and hard chest became my favorite place to be. And just like I could never help myself from adding a few extra chocolate chips to my cupcake batter, I knew I could never deny myself a taste of Tate for as long as he was willing to give it to me.

I felt a little off balance when the kiss ended, and Tate stared at me like he knew exactly how I felt.

"Um...right...we should...*fuck*," I stuttered.

"We should... fuck?" Tate said, his lips quirking into a teasing smile.

I leaned my forehead against his chest and took a deep breath. He kissed the top of my head and ran his hands over my hair, caressing the back of my neck.

"Come on, Tight Buns, show me your secret spot," he said.

We walked the length of the field and then turned away from it into an overgrown part of Reed's property.

The water tower wasn't exactly a secret spot, since Reed had told me about it, and knew I always came here every time I picked up an order, but he didn't allow visitors this far into the farm.

"Is this safe?" Tate asked, shaking the rusty iron stairs that led up to the tower.

"Yup. First one up gets dibs on the goody bag," I said, climbing up.

"That's not fair," he said, trying to pull me down, but I was too quick for him.

"There's another set of stairs on the other side."

"What, and miss staring at your perfect ass all the way up?"

I groaned.

When we got to the top, we sat on the edge with our back to the tower and our feet dangling down.

A hundred feet off the ground, the individual shrubs of lavender became seamless rows of purple.

No matter how many times I'd come up here, it always took my breath away. Each season showcased the lavender in a different way; each year had its own effect on the crops because of the weather. If I was a religious man, this place here would be my church.

"That was a good idea for the wedding favors," I said, breaking our silence.

"Really?"

"Yes, I told you Tristan would like it."

"And you?"

I grabbed the gift bag and opened a small packet of lemon and lavender cookies. They smelled divine.

"Indy?"

I sighed, not needing to look at Tate to know his eyes were on me, and put the cookies down.

"I was going to have small pots of lavender and apricot honey as my wedding favors."

"Were... going to?"

"The wedding didn't happen."

Tate put his hand on my back and ran it up and down.

"It's okay, it was a long time ago, and yes, you can ask. He waited until the week before the wedding to tell me he didn't think he loved me anymore. He didn't want to be stuck in a small town forever. Then he left. End of story."

I let out a laugh. I've never needed to tell this story to anyone before because everyone in Chester Falls had seen it happen. The preparations. The betrayal. The fallout.

Funny enough, it wasn't as hard as I thought. Yes, when Tate had suggested the honey pots as wedding favors I'd been transported back to that time momentarily, and then there was a part of me that wondered if it was a bad omen. But just like the honey was sweet with its unique flavor, so was Tristan and Ben's relationship. It was the perfect gift.

"Can I ask you something?" Tate said.

"Of course."

"You seem to be so excited about the wedding. I'd have

thought being jilted nearly at the altar would make someone a lot more..."

"Bitter? Angry? Disillusioned?" I gave Tate a cookie and took one for me. "I was all those things for a while. But I'm a baker. Weddings are part of my job. Besides, what can I say? I'm a hopeless romantic. Maybe that time wasn't meant to be, but one day..."

I pulled the bag of cookies away from Tate when he tried to steal another one. I was telling him my screwed up history, so I deserved to command the cookies.

"How about you? I could be wrong, but I get the feeling weddings, or maybe marriage, are not your thing," I said.

"I'm a divorce attorney. I see the worst of people that once swore in front of a minister to love and cherish each other forever." He shrugged.

"There are lots of happily married divorce attorneys. What gives?"

I looked inside the goody bag, and there was a bar of lavender-infused chocolate. God, I was going to marry Reed.

"I'll share the chocolate with you," I teased, shaking the bar up in front of his face.

"You don't play fair," he said.

"If I didn't play fair, we'd be doing this naked. Now talk."

He laughed, shaking his head, but then his face took on a more serious expression.

"My parents divorced when Tristan and I were ten. It came out of nowhere. We were a happy family until...we weren't. Tristan and I got separated in the divorce because my dad threatened to not give my mom any alimony unless he had custody of one of us. She'd been a stay-at-home mom and hadn't worked for years, so she was afraid to be out there on her own and took the deal. Tristan stayed with our mom, and I had to live with our dad."

"Fuck, Tate, that must have been horrible."

"I cried for days. Tristan and I missed each other like crazy.

We even had to go to different schools because my dad moved us out of the district. Weeks later, my dad moved his girlfriend in, and as they say, once a cheater..."

My heart ached for Tate. To watch his family break up, especially be apart from his twin.

"Unlike my mother, who divorced him as soon as she found out about the cheating, his girlfriend loved the lifestyle he provided more than her self respect."

"Are they still together?"

"I think so. I moved out when I left for college and haven't spoken to my dad since."

Tate leaned back against the water tower and closed his eyes. His light brown hair was a little longer since we'd met. I ran my hand through its softness, and my heart skipped a beat when he smiled.

"My first boyfriend in college cheated on me, and so did the second and third," he said. "I was so desperate to be loved by someone. I was too clingy and wanted so badly to prove to myself that I wasn't a cheater like my dad, I ended up being like his girlfriend."

He turned his head to face me and grabbed my hand, kissing my palm before resting it on his chest.

"Indy, I want you more than I've ever wanted someone. I think I did from the moment I saw you, but I can't give you what you need. You deserve someone who wants a relationship, who wants to go down the aisle and profess their undying love for you in front of all your family and friends."

I used the heel of my foot to help me up and then turned to straddle Tate. He put his hands on my waist and gripped tight, but I knew the safety railings along the tower were strong and there was no way we'd fall down.

"Why don't we let *me* worry about what I want out of life and focus on what I want now?" I said, running my hands over his chest, feeling the ridges of his muscles and his heart beating fast underneath.

"What's that?"

"You."

Two perfect kisses. I had two perfect kisses I could frame and hang up on the walls of my memory. Now I wanted more, and I was tired of fighting it.

I pulled my shirt off and then helped Tate out of his.

"Fuck, Tate, you're..."

"I'm what, Tightbuns? Hard for you? Dying to see you come apart? Damn right I am."

I laughed until I felt his erection beneath me.

Tate put his hands under my ass and raised me up so his face was lined up perfectly with my chest. He flattened his tongue on my left nipple and tugged the barbell with his teeth.

"Tate!" I sucked in a breath. "Fuck."

TATE

y name coming out of Indy's lips as I tugged the piercing on his nipple was officially the best sound in the world. Forget best-selling albums, sell-out concerts, or music awards; nothing could ever compare.

"Why only one?" I asked, moving to the neglected nipple.

"Because the first one fucking hurt," he said, tugging on my hair to tilt my head up for a kiss.

The rickety wood of the old tower cracked in synchrony with Indy's thrusts against me. My cock was painfully hard, and my brain was going through all the possible options for fast relief, all of which required a lot less clothing.

"Indy," I said against his mouth. "What do you want, baby."

"You. Everything. Now."

His hands ran down my chest toward the button of my jeans, but I stopped him.

"Indy, I don't want to hurt you."

"How fucking big are you?"

"Big enough, but you know what I mean. We can't take this back."

He looked straight at me and put both his hands on my face.

"I would rather have the memory of a single perfect time with you than not knowing, Tate."

"Okay."

He stood up but kept a foot on either side of me. I helped him out of his shoes while he worked on the buttons of his jeans.

"Can people see us up here?" I asked.

"No, customers aren't allowed this way, and staff don't come around at this time."

"Put your hands on the wall, Indigo."

I waited until he did and then helped him out of his jeans and underwear. His cock was long and hard. Tiny beads of pre-cum leaked from the slit.

"Tate," he begged.

"It's okay, baby. I'll give you everything you need."

I wrapped my hand around his length and teased his slit with my tongue before sucking on his crown. He fought against the instinct to push himself against me, but I was having none of that. I didn't want self-control. I wanted Indy to fall apart.

"Suck on my finger. Make it nice and wet," I said, raising my hand up. "I'm going to make sure you're ready for me."

With my free hand, I undid the button on my jeans to free my erection. The early afternoon breeze was both relief and torture. My cock was oversensitive from being constricted for so long that it was downright painful.

As soon as Indy released my finger, I took his cock in my mouth again and used both hands to open up his ass cheeks and tease my way in.

"Fuck, oh god, fuck," he shouted.

I moaned around his cock until his legs were shaking under the weight of his impending orgasm. At the very last minute, I removed my finger from his hole, tugged on his balls, and wrapped a hand at the base of his cock to stop him from coming.

His legs gave out, and he slid all the way down until he was on my lap again.

"I fucking hate you," he said, trying to catch his breath.

I slammed my mouth onto his for a hungry kiss. His spit-covered cock slid against mine so perfectly I was the one struggling to breathe.

"Need inside you," I breathed out.

He reached out for his jeans and took a condom and packet of lube from his wallet.

"Look at you, boy scout" I teased as he opened up the condom and rolled it down my length.

"Nope, just a horny baker."

He opened the lube and added some to his fingers before reaching behind him. I loved that he was so desperate for me he was prepping himself. My cock twitched against my stomach in anticipation of being inside Indy.

I took the rest of the lube and coated it generously on my cock.

Indy raised himself and then slowly lowered onto me.

"Look at me," he said. "I need you to know you're with me."

"How could I forget, Indy. How could I?"

My words became choked as the intense heat of Indy's body and the pressure of his tightness made it hard to breathe.

He was totally in control... of the pace... of me.

Within a few thrusts, he was fully seated on my cock.

"It feels so good, Tate. So full."

He raised himself up and back down again, his eyes so dark they were no longer blue.

I pulled his hairband off and ran my hands through his hair as the soft, wavy tendrils fell down his back.

Indy was a piece of art with his slim body, milky white skin, long hair, and sexy as fuck pierced nipple.

He was everything all of my previous lovers hadn't been, and I was only scratching the surface. There was so much more of Indy to uncover, like a layer cake, except he was much sweeter.

"I'm so close, Tate," he breathed out.

"Me, too, baby."

I reached for his cock, but he pushed my hand away and shook his head. He leaned back on the railings of the water tower and held his arms open wide, gripping the hard metal with his hands.

With his head held back, hair hanging over the railing, and his back a perfect arch as he bounced up and down on my cock, Indy was the most beautiful sight I'd ever seen.

His movements became less controlled as he impaled himself on me, the desperate sounds going straight to my cock.

I was so close I had to bite the inside of my cheek. Indy needed to come first, in more ways than one, but in this moment, my sanity and my reason for being depended on watching him come apart.

"Take everything, Indy. Make me yours."

He raised his head forward, and stared straight at me.

With his eyes on mine, his hair wild and flowing in the late spring lavender-scented breeze and with the hum of the bees in the background, Indy let go.

My last thought before I spilled into the condom was how Indy had been right and also very wrong.

Our one time was better than perfect, but there was no way we could have just the one time.

Indy became a pile of soft noodles on top of me, not even noticing as my limp cock slowly left his body.

"Remind me why we didn't do this on day one," he said.

"I needed to grow on you."

He let out a laugh. "Oh, you did, big boy, you *so* did."

"I hate to ruin the moment because I could stay here with you on top of me for a while..."

"But..." he said, looking up at me with a sated smile and still flushed skin. I couldn't resist stealing another kiss.

"But my ass is getting numb, and you're naked...above a field."

He sighed. "I think we gave mother nature quite a show."

"Reed is going to have some horny bees on his hands. Honey production is going to soar."

"He's going to beg us to come here every week for a repeat."

"You won't hear any complaints from me," I said. "But maybe we'll bring a cushion next time."

"And more food. That chocolate is mine."

I laughed and then groaned as he lifted up from me and I saw the mess we were in.

"I think I saw a tea cloth in the gift bag," Indy said.

"I'm sure this isn't what Reed had in mind when he put the gift bag together."

I grabbed the tea cloth and cleaned us both before removing the condom tying a knot and wrapping it in the cloth.

We walked back to the car mostly in silence. Indy had one arm around my waist as he devoured his hard-earned chocolate bar, and I held mine over his shoulder. It wasn't awkward, I didn't lack words to say, nor was I trying to find a way to flee. I also had no inclination to think too much into it. At least for now.

"Um, Tate?"

"Yeah?"

"Are you going back to Boston tonight?"

"No, Tom is measuring me for the suit tomorrow."

Indy went quiet as he finished his chocolate bar and put the wrapper in the bag. We were back at his car, so he pretended to be busy looking for his keys.

I pulled them out from his back pocket and pushed him gently against the car, tilting his head up so I could see his eyes.

"Was there a reason for your question?"

"Um, are you staying at the motel again? I heard...I mean, um...last week there was a break-in. It was in the local paper."

I tilted my head and gave him a teasing smile, putting a little more of my weight on him.

"Are you worried about my safety?"

"No, well yes, but..." He let out a frustrated and totally adorable huff. "Do you want to stay over at my place?"

I nuzzled his neck and sucked on his skin until I was sure there would be a mark.

"Can you feel that?" I asked.

"Nghnn, feel...um...yes."

"I'd love to stay with you. You go to bed early, don't you?"

He moved his head to face me, but I couldn't read his expression.

"Yes, I'm working tomorrow. You don't have to go to bed with me. I mean, um, we don't have to. You can go to bed whenever you like. Whatever time. Yeah, whatev—"

I stopped his mumble with a kiss and only stopped when I felt his dick hardening against mine.

"Baby, the only reason I asked was so I can tell you to drive fast so we can get you home, fed, and ravished in time for your bedtime," I said.

He bit his lip. "Ravished, huh?"

I winked and dangled the car keys in front of him.

INDY

It was unusual that I beat my alarm clock, especially by fifteen minutes. Especially when it wasn't even four in the morning. More unusual than that was feeling rested and like I'd had the best night's sleep in a long time.

A sleepy groan came from my very gorgeous and very naked companion. Tate was sprawled out on his belly with a heavy arm over me. The bedsheets had ridden down and were tangled around his legs.

If it wasn't so dark in the room, I'd take a picture of him. Defined muscles, enough hair to make it sexy without looking like a Sasquatch, and two dimples leading to the most perfect butt I'd ever seen.

He tightened his hold on me, pulling me closer and breathing me in before placing a kiss on my shoulder.

"Hmm, what time is it?"

His raspy voice was doing all the things to my already awake cock. Tate was hard against my leg.

Ugh, fucking work.

"It's time for me to get up and for you to grab a few more hours' sleep. Dream of me," I said, moving to kiss his cheek and then get up, except Tate had other plans, and I ended up pinned to the bed under him.

My breath caught as he rutted against me.

"I told you once wasn't enough," he said, his mouth feasting on mine like it was breakfast.

"I know. I was here for the other three times last night before I finally passed out. Surely that must be some kind of record."

"I'll look it up."

I chuckled and wrapped my legs around his waist. I probably still had enough lube in me and the condoms were a small stretch away.

Tate increased his pace. My body hummed in anticipation of an orgasm.

"Indy..." Tate rasped.

"Keep going, I'm so close."

And that's when my fucking, cockblocking, traitor of an alarm clock decided to go off.

"No, don't stop," I whined, as Tate stopped both the alarm clock and his thrusts.

"I don't want to make you late, baby."

"Punctuality is overrated," I said, relenting and getting up.

I grabbed a new pair of boxer shorts and put them on. When I turned to look for my work jeans, Tate already had his on.

"What are you doing?"

"What does it look like I'm doing?"

My stomach sank, but I managed to keep my face neutral. I knew we wouldn't have a repeat, but him leaving before the sun was even up left a bitter taste in my mouth.

Okay, so in the past, I'd always been the one to leave early. My hookups knew that and didn't mind. We'd gotten off, so grabbing a nap and leaving early suited us both.

But Tate wasn't a hookup. He was becoming a friend. One

that I was insanely attracted to and had explosive chemistry with, but a friend nonetheless.

"Hey, what's up?" he asked.

"Um, nothing, just running through the stuff I have to do before I open up. Jake's off today."

I avoided making eye contact as I looked for a clean work shirt in the drawer.

Tate came from behind me. He ran his hands through my loose hair and then I felt a hairbrush.

A stupid frog lodged itself in my throat. I looked up to the mirror above the dresser to see Tate's look of concentration as he tied up my hair in a perfect bun.

As soon as he was done, I grabbed my keys for Spilled Beans.

"Just close the door on your way out."

Each step down the stairs from my apartment felt heavy. The smell of baked goods that was ingrained in the walls of my coffee shop failed to make me smile, which annoyed me more than anything.

I turned the industrial coffee machine on to warm up and went to the kitchen where I had a smaller one I used for my morning coffee.

While the coffee brewed, I looked at the notice board to see if there were any updates from Jake.

I saw a couple of bills I needed to pay, which could wait until Monday, and there was a sticky note saying we'd run out of chocolate chip cookie dough so he hadn't been able to bake any more fresh cookies.

Ah-ha, there it was, just what I needed. There was also an order for my signature vanilla and chocolate ganache cupcakes. I could work on those after I got everything else going.

I was going to turn the radio on when the tall, sexy figure leaning against the wall scared the sprinkles out of me.

"Fuck, Tate. What are you doing here?"

His eyes narrowed.

"Why did you run out of your place like it was on fire?" he asked.

"Like you said, I have work to do. You said you were leaving, so..."

"No, I didn't."

"Yes, you did," I argued.

"No," he said, coming closer to me, "I didn't."

"You put your jeans on," I argued as if it made any sense, which now, come to think of it, it didn't.

"I can take them off again if you like." His smile was teasing, and I couldn't help a small smile. Tiny, barely noticeable.

"Indy," he said, placing a hand on either side of my face and tilting it up. "I wasn't leaving. I was getting dressed to help you."

He was?

I was officially an idiot.

"What time do you open?" he asked.

"Eight."

He looked at the clock on the wall.

"So we have four hours...and two people can get the job done faster, right?"

"Um, yes?"

What was he getting at?

"In that case, I think I need to have breakfast first."

"Okay, there's some oatmeal in the cupboard and milk in the fridg...what are you doing?"

Tate walked me back until I hit the kitchen island and then got on his knees.

"I'm more of a protein man," he said, his blue eyes shiny and promising. "Did you know protein is good to build up muscle..."

"Uh-huh..."

He opened the top button on my jeans and palmed my growing erection.

"And last night you told me how much you like my muscles."

I swallowed and closed my eyes as he pulled the zipper down, pressed his nose against my crotch, and inhaled.

"Fuuuck."

"Not now, baby, but I'm going to suck you like a hoover until you're nice and relaxed."

He pulled my jeans and boxer shorts down only enough to expose my cock and balls, and before I expressed my undying agreement at this turn of events, he licked a path from the root to the head of my cock.

My legs nearly buckled under my weight so I had to lock my knees and lean back on the counter for support. Tate did suck like a high powered hoover until I was cursing like a sailor and spilling down his throat.

He didn't stop lavishing my cock with attention until I was over-sensitive but clean enough that he tucked me back in and zipped me up like nothing had happened.

"I think coffee is ready," he said, getting up and picking two cups from the counter and filling them. "You take yours black, right?"

I nodded, still too lightheaded for words.

Three and a half hours later, Tate was covered in flour, had buttercream all over his face, and his hair was white from the bag of powdered sugar he accidentally burst, but I was for once ahead of schedule and had time for breakfast. The food kind.

"I suppose I should feed you as a thanks for the help." And then clarified when he quirked a brow. "Food, like the nourishing kind."

"I'd love one of your bagels, thanks."

The kitchen was a mess, but I didn't care. I could clean it later after the morning rush.

I grabbed two fresh bagels, cream cheese, and smoked

salmon and sat next to Tate on a corner of the island he'd cleared.

"Is baking always this messy?" he asked.

I laughed. "No."

"These are really good," he said, taking a bite of his bagel.

"You sure you got enough cream cheese there?"

He grinned and took another bite.

"You're an animal," I said.

"You know it, baby." He winked. "Did you always want to be a baker?"

"Yes. My parents are total hippies, so everything we had was homemade. Every day at school I was jealous that my friends had these delicious looking cookies in their lunch boxes. My mom was a hopeless baker, so she'd get bread from the bakery for sandwiches, but her rule bending didn't extend to sugary treats."

Tate smiled. "So you decided to try your own?"

"Yup. We had my grandmother's recipe books on a shelf, so I started experimenting."

"Did you have long hair then?" he asked, pushing a loose wave behind my ear.

"No, I didn't let it grow until I finished high school."

Tate ran his hand over his beard and took a breath. "I guess you need to go open up."

I looked at the clock. He was right.

I stood up and kissed him. "Don't be afraid of Tom, there's no bite to his bark. Hell, there's no bark to his bark."

TATE

"*C*an I move already?" I asked, my frustration building up.

"Not yet. I've got to get this right. Stop being fussy."

"We've been at this for hours."

"It's been twenty minutes."

"Forty-five."

"Okay, you're all in. You can move now...slowly, though."

I turned around to look in the floor to ceiling mirror. Sure enough, the shirt fit perfectly. Well, as soon as it was put together with thread instead of pins.

Tom stood back with a bunch of pins stuck between his teeth and narrowed his eyes.

"What?" I asked.

"Mmm...not sure. There's something missing."

"My trousers?"

Why the fuck did I have to undress down to my boxer shorts to have a shirt fitted?

Tom chuckled and took a sip of his blue cocktail.

"Should you be drinking while sticking pins into my body?"

"Don't worry, Old Man. It's non-alcoholic," my brother said, walking into Fabulize and taking a seat on the couch.

I had plenty of made to measure suits because of my size, but I'd never seen a fitting room as spacious, welcoming, and comfortable as Tom's. He even had a heavy curtain pulled across for privacy.

"Did you have to take all your clothes off when you got measured?" I asked him.

Tristan took a sip of the cocktail Tom had made for me and pulled a face. "Jeez, Tom, how much sugar is in this?"

"Only enough to give you a buzz," he said. "I didn't have time to bake my brownies. Wren came home early yesterday and we...well, you know what boys who love boys do."

I snorted. Oh yes, I did know. I'd spent last evening doing all the things boys who love boys do.

"Where did you stay last night?" Tristan asked.

Fuck.

"At the motel, like last time."

"You know you could have stayed with us, right?" Tristan looked...disappointed?

"Yeah, I know, but I've grown out of hearing other people's sex noises when I left college," I said.

"Oooh, who's making sex noises?" Wren said, coming in and sitting next to Tristan. "And why are you naked?"

I gave him a look that said "ask your boyfriend."

"Tom?" Wren said.

Tom poked his head from behind me where it seemed he was working on making this the tightest shirt in the history of tight shirts.

"Yes, Sprinkles?" Tom said in a sugary sweet voice that seemed to work on Wren if his whipped face was anything to go by.

"Okay, hotcakes. I think I got it. Let's get this off and try the slacks," Tom said, unpinning the shirt carefully, leaving me standing in my boxer shorts with an audience.

"Don't you guys have somewhere else to be?"

"Nope," Wren said, looking as appreciative of my state of undress as his boyfriend.

"Yes, actually. Ben's busy next door, so I'm going to grab him a coffee," my brother said. "Does anyone want one of Indy's buns?"

"No one's having Indy's buns," I said too quickly and *not* inside my head.

Three pairs of eyes stared at me. "Um, I meant...uh, I stopped by earlier, and he'd run out already."

"He's probably baked more since. See you later." Tristan left, and Wren sat back, sipping from my cocktail.

Tom was still staring at me. I looked down. "Is there something wrong? You didn't prick me this time, if you're worried."

"Nope...nothing wrong."

He helped me into the slacks, which fortunately had a lot fewer pins.

"Tate, do you mind if I ask you a question?" Tom said.

I laughed. "You don't look like the type of person who'd ever be shy about anything, so go on."

Wren got up and placed a soft kiss on Tom's lips. "There's more to my Angel than meets the eye, Tate. Don't let him trick you into a false sense of security. You'll end up spilling your worst secrets to him." He gave me a pat on the shoulder and left.

Unlikely.

Something told me they were all very protective of each other, and with Indy being the single one, I'd be in trouble if anyone ever knew we'd hooked up.

"You wanted to ask me a question?" I said.

Tom knelt down with his pins once again between his teeth as he measured the length of my legs.

"You like Indy's buns."

"That's not a question..."

"I know, I'm just letting you know...Indy's buns are

special. The best you can have, and they must be cherished as the special, rare delicacy they are."

What the fuck does that mean?

After another long hour of standing still to avoid being pierced to death, I was finally free from Tom's claws. Okay, so it hadn't been that bad, but I'd left Fabulize with the distinct feeling that I'd been warned, and not sure against what.

The line to get inside Spilled Beans was going as strong as when I'd left earlier, so I decided to drop by Bookmarked first.

There was a small line for the checkout, which was manned by Ben's part-time helper, but otherwise, the store was quiet. Ben was by the window with a notepad in hand looking worried.

"Hey, everything okay?" I asked.

"Oh, hi, Tate. How was your fitting?"

"Boring in parts and far too exciting in others, but I'm grateful Tom decided to use Tristan's measurements for me. I think he only needs to make some adjustments and I'll be set."

"Yeah, Tom's great."

Ben looked at his notepad and then again toward the square.

"Where's Tristan?"

"Oh, one of his clients had a delivery, and he was so excited to see the fabric. He'll be back later."

That was my brother. He'd always been the more creative of the two of us. I liked rules, knowing what was right and wrong, which was why law had been the best career path for me.

Tristan liked bending the rules. Not by misbehaving, but if there was a rule that two things didn't go together, he'd always find a way.

Maybe that was why he seemed so happy. He'd turned his life around after the shit we'd been dealt.

"You looked worried," I said to Ben.

He sighed. "I've been thinking about my vows, and I realized that Tristan has given me everything. Before him, I was drifting along. He encouraged me to follow my dreams, to write, to be a better businessman. He makes me feel like I'm the only person that matters to him. He became friends with my friends; my parents love him. He's...he's my whole world." Ben's voice broke a little. "I don't know what I have to offer to him. What if I'm not enough and he realizes that living in Chester Falls is boring, or that he wants to expand his business and move to the city. What if he stops loving me?"

A small tear left ran down Ben's cheek. I looked around, and fortunately, all the customers had left and the kid was busy putting books away on the other side of the store.

I placed my hand on Ben's shoulder. I had no clue what to say or how to make him feel better. I was totally the wrong person for this kind of thing. What could I say? That I didn't believe in marriage? That all relationships were doomed to fail because every single person I loved had had their heart broken?

Except, my gut feeling told me Ben and Tristan *were* the real deal, the exception that proved the rule.

"Ben, my brother loves you more than anything. I know we've lived apart most of our lives, but he's my twin. I *know* him. Whatever you give him, it's enough, and it'll always be enough."

If I ever found someone who looks at me like you look at each other, maybe, just maybe, I'd change my mind about relationships.

I was taken by surprise when Ben hugged me.

"Thank you, Tate. I'm really happy that you're in Tristan's life again."

"Me, too. So, are you going to recommend something good for me to read, or shall I go browse the legal section again?" I joked.

"A. Lawton has a new book out. It's like the gay version of *The Wedding Date*, but so much better."

I bought the book and talked in all the right places, but

since the conversation with Ben, my head had been all over the place.

Tristan came back from his client not long after and suggested having lunch with Tom and Wren at Spilled Beans. Suddenly, I felt like there wasn't enough air in Chester Falls for me to breathe.

I made up an excuse that I needed to go back to Boston and left.

It wasn't until I was halfway to Boston that I stopped for gas and got my phone out.

Tate: Are you home?
Harrison: No, I'm at a twink orgy.
Tate: I knew it!
Harrison: Just a regular Saturday afternoon.
Tate: Can I drop by?
Harrison: Sure, but I'm out of beer.
Tate: Forget it then.
Harrison: You're so fickle.
Tate: The ficklest.
Harrison: That's not a word.
Tate: It is now. I'll bring beer. And cake.
Harrison: Oh dear...
Tate: Yeah...

I looked at Indy's unread text on my phone, but I wasn't ready to reply just yet.

INDY

$\mathcal{W}$as it me, or was everyone super happy today?

Okay, it was totally me, because Mr. Jensen was still the same grumpy old man as he ordered his usual coffee—black, no sugar—and one sugar cookie. As if I'd forget the only thing he'd ever bought from me in the years since I'd opened.

It didn't matter one bit. I'd managed two batches of cinnamon buns, baked three trays of cookies, and had everything lined up to bake the cupcakes later.

If only I had this much energy every single day.

"You're in a good mood. Did the wind finally change?"

I laughed and went around the cake display counter to give my mom a hug. If only she knew how the wind had changed.

"You look stunning mom."

"What, these old rags? And don't change the subject."

I was definitely trying to change the subject, but I couldn't deny my mother's sense of style. It was as if she didn't have a particular age. Pamela Birch looked as great in a summer dress as she did in well-worn dungarees and tie-dye shirts.

"Never, mother. Would you like a slice of cake? Or perhaps a cinnamon roll?"

She gave me her "don't bullshit your mother" look.

"Let's save the dance for another time. I was upstairs."

I groaned.

"Please tell me you didn't buy me any more dick stuff, and *please* tell me you didn't go inside my room."

We were interrupted by a customer, so I had the pleasure to imagine in my head the possible answers to my question while I created the perfect caramel latte and cut a slice of chocolate cake. Thank god the customer wanted to sit outside.

As soon as he was out of the door, I turned to my mom who was trying to look innocent, which just got my heart beating a little faster, and not in a good way.

"Mom?"

She huffed.

"Well, it's not my fault. Your brother—"

I put my hand up. "Just tell me what kind of dick I have in my apartment."

"A painting."

"How big?"

She decided now was a good time to inspect the cakes on display.

"Could I have a slice of—"

"Mom!"

"It's rather um...large."

"Stay here, and don't touch *anything*."

I ran upstairs.

"You're out of ice cream," my brother said, poking his head out of the kitchen archway.

"Where is it?"

"Your bedroom," he said, coming out of the kitchen eating an apple.

"Don't you have food at your place?" I asked, going to my

room and feeling my blood pressure increasing to astronomical levels.

"Duh, yeah, but yours is free."

"No, it isn't. And...Oh. Fuck. Me. What the fuck, Sage."

Was it still illegal to kill your family? I'd need to ask Tate about it because my family was dead. Like D.E.A.D.

Who the fuck buys someone a painting of a penis? No, let me correct. Who buys someone a *giant* painting of an erect penis?

"What the fuck am I supposed to do with this, Sage?"

"Masturbate while you look at it?"

I pushed him and he fell into my bed, bouncing off of it quickly with a disgusted face.

"Ew, I don't want to touch your sex-filled bed sheets."

"Grow up," I yelled, although now I was secretly pleased that my sheets were indeed sex-filled. Three times sex-filled.

"Get out of my place," I said.

"Can I grab a slice of—"

"No!"

I took a deep breath and counted to twenty before I went downstairs to the coffee shop.

It was okay. Maybe I could sell or donate the painting to someone who really loved dick more than me.

"You must visit us soon," my mom said as soon as I was back downstairs.

"Not a chance. Do you realize this is why I can't bring anyone here? How am I meant to have a relationship if I can't bring a guy home without fear of being attacked by inflatable dicks or opening the fridge to a giant jelly dick? And now a painting?"

"Oh, don't give me that 'I can't bring anyone here' excuse. I could smell it as soon as I got in. Why do you think I came straight back down?"

I ran my hands over my face and took another deep breath.

"We must go now. The Tindalls have invited us for dinner, and we mustn't be late."

Thankfully, lunchtime on Saturday was always quiet because I needed a moment to recover from this. I picked up my phone, but Tate hadn't answered my message.

He'd probably need something to eat when Tom finally let him go.

I put aside one of the bread rolls I baked earlier to make him a sandwich and started condensing the few cupcakes and cinnamon buns I had left to sell.

I hated seeing the display cabinet bare, but toward the end of the day, I also didn't like waste.

Usually, my last customers got to take some extra home with them.

One look up to the square, and I knew I'd have nothing left in a short moment.

"I hope you have enough bread rolls, cake, and coffee to feed the troops," Wren said, leading the way, followed by Tom, Tristan, Ben, Hannah, Ellie, and baby Charlotte in her rainbow stroller.

"Prepare to be hungry a little longer because this is Uncle Indy and Princess Charlie cuddle time," I said, going straight for the stroller.

I unbuckled Charlotte and held her to my chest. "Hello, Cupcake, what can I get you? I guess you're not into coffee just yet, right? I'm afraid I don't serve booby milk." She looked up at me with her big blue eyes and smiled. "Oh my god, she smiled!"

"It's probably wind," Ellie said.

"Nope, I'm her favorite uncle and she knows it."

"Not in a million sparkly years," Tom said. "She's already the best-dressed girl in town."

"You're all wrong," Tristan said. "She's going to be like her daddy, super smart, and she'll write best-seller books before she's five."

Hannah and Ellie both looked at Ben, and Ellie gave him a hug. It was great seeing my friends all happy, but what Ben had done for Ellie and Hannah to help them have Charlotte melted my heart a thousand times over.

Charlotte already had three parents, a step-parent, two sets of grandparents, and all the uncles in the world to make sure she was the happiest little girl.

"Right, I'm getting all emotional and broody here. Hannah, take your daughter away from me before I kidnap her and give me your food orders."

I was so used to the Saturday lunchtime invasion from my friends, that it wasn't until I went back behind the counter that I realized Tate wasn't with them.

Had he gone back to Boston? I assumed he'd stay in Chester Falls the whole weekend.

"Do you need any help?" Tom asked.

I didn't even notice him getting up and approaching the counter.

"Oh, no thanks, I've got it under control. I've fed you all countless times before."

He hummed but didn't go back to the table.

"All okay?" I asked.

"Tate was here today," he said.

I looked at the group who were cooing over Charlotte.

"Oh really? I suppose he was being measured for the wedding suit, right?"

Tom tilted his head and put a finger on his chin.

"So you didn't see him then?"

"Me? Nope." Fuck, I hated lying and already felt my skin heat up.

"That's interesting, because he said he was here earlier buying a cinnamon bun."

I gave Tom a pleading look.

"Oh my god, you horny, lucky devil," Tom whispered excitedly. "And he's a big boy, too."

"It's not like that," I whispered back, "and how do you know?"

"I had my hands all up his business today. Trust me, honey, I noticed." He came even closer. "I bet he had his hands all up in your business, too, last night."

I was full-on blushing now and these sandwiches were never going to be finished.

Tom raised two fingers and rolled his eyes.

I shook my head and raised three.

"Holy Coco, Indy."

I shrugged. "It had been a while."

"So what, are you guys a thing?"

"No, please don't tell anyone. We haven't talked about anything yet. He was really sweet and helped me this morning, but I haven't heard from him since."

"Tristan said he had to go back to Boston. Something about work."

"Oh."

I didn't know what to think, and after getting it so wrong this morning, I didn't want to make any assumptions. Maybe he did have a work thing. He'd probably message me later.

Tom grabbed two of the plates with the sandwiches I'd already made, and said, "I won't tell anything, not even to Wren, okay. I swear it on my love of Coco...the Channel and my cat. If you want to talk, just say the word, okay?"

I smiled and nodded, knowing there was no need for it. Tate and I weren't an item. We'd had fun together caused by insane chemistry. He didn't owe me anything.

Oh, I see you're now lying to yourself, too, Indy. Fantastic.

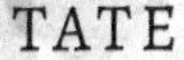

TATE

"*H*ey, Ladybug."

"Uncle Tate, I'm going on a vacation to the beach."

"Oh really? Have you packed your swimsuit?" I smiled as the picture on the phone moved around and I heard Megan speak to her mom.

"Uncle Tate, are you there?"

"I am, Ladybug."

"Mommy said yes."

"I guess you're all ready then. Have lots of fun."

"I will," she said, and then ran off leaving the phone behind.

Stella appeared a moment later.

"Thanks, Tate. She wouldn't go to bed before we called you."

"That's okay. You know I never mind talking to her. You have a good vacation."

I smiled and ended the call as Harrison came back out from his kitchen with two beers in hand.

"You're really great with her. You sure you don't want kids?

"Yeah, I'm sure. I get to spoil her and then give her back to you."

He snorted.

"So... The guy you met... the other best man..."

"Yeah."

"I thought you were just friends."

"We are...were...are...fuck!" I sighed and ran my hand over my beard.

Indy had done that a lot last night. Between our rounds of scorching hot sex, we'd talked about anything and everything. He seemed fixated on smoothing out my beard and tracing my lips while I constantly ran my fingers through his long hair.

"Okay, so you fucked, and then you did what you always do. You bolted."

"What? I don't do that."

Harrison gave me a pointed look.

"You know I don't do relationships, Hare. The guys I'm with know the score. What's the point of staying if it's not going anywhere?"

"I take it you were upfront with this guy."

"Yes, I told him everything, including the reason I don't do relationships."

"But then you stayed the night."

"Yes...?"

"And you helped him with his work in the morning."

"Yes."

"And you said you'd be back later."

"Fuck...I'm a jackass."

Harrison grabbed my phone from the coffee table and threw it at me.

"What the hell do I say?" I asked, staring at the phone.

"How about you start with an apology and go from there? I'll go check on the pasta sauce and give you some privacy."

It was my turn to give him a pointed look.

"Okay, okay. I'll be listening through the door, but you

won't see me, so pretend you're on your own," he said as he walked to the kitchen.

I unlocked and read the message he sent me earlier.

Indy: I have a new dick gift from my family.

The next message came some time after the first.

Indy: How good are you defending a potential murderer? Or is it manslaughter if I was provoked?
Indy: Will you visit me in jail?

My thumb hovered over the keyboard, but I stopped myself from replying to the message. I pulled up his number and hit call.

"Hello?"

"Indy?"

There was a moment of silence on the other side.

"Tate."

"Yeah, it's me. Um, look—"

"Tristan said you had a work thing. Did you get back to Boston in time to fix it? I hope you did. It's a shame you missed meeting Charlotte. That's Ellie and Hannah's baby. Ellie works with Ben, but she's on maternity now and—"

"Indy," I interrupted. "I'm sorry I left without saying anything."

"That's okay. You don't owe me an explanation. We're not dating or anything, right?"

I breathed out. "Right. But still, I should have said something."

"Why didn't you?" His voice was steady, hard to interpret through the phone. I stared at the screen wanting to switch the call to video, but I knew it was a bad idea, so I put the cell back to my ear.

"Because I wanted to see you again," I confessed.

"That makes no sense."

"I know."

"Can we still be friends?" he asked.

"Yes. I'd like that very much."

"Okay. So, um, I guess I'll see you around, you know...as friends."

I smiled, wishing I could reach out through the phone and touch him. "Yes, I guess you will."

Harrison came back out from the kitchen with two plates piled up with pasta and meatballs.

I didn't think I was that hungry earlier, but the smell of the tomato sauce opened up the well inside me, and I felt like I could eat anything Harrison put in front of me.

~

Tate: What's on tonight?

Indy: *The Bodyguard.*

Tate: Kevin Costner and an amazing soundtrack. I'm in.

Indy: I liked him better in *Robin Hood.*

Tate: Dibs on Christian Slater.

Indy: Christian/Kevin threesome. Damn.

I laughed at the gif he sent of Blanche Devereaux from the Golden Girls fanning herself and set myself a reminder for when I got home later.

It had been a month since I'd seen Indy. I missed him, but we seemed to have reached a good balance in our friendship. We had our movie nights when we watched the same romantic movie together and had a running commentary by text.

And then there was the wedding stuff, on which I hung my head in shame because Indy had done most of it. Work had picked up, and with my boss finally acknowledging the opening of a new partner seat, I hadn't had any time off in weeks.

"Hey, wanna grab a beer after work?" Harrison said, poking his head in my office.

"Can't, it's movie night tonight."

He nodded and gave me a strange look. I didn't have time to ask him what was up because my new client was going to be here in ten minutes and I needed a coffee. Stat.

My phone buzzed, and I picked it up expecting to see Indy's latest message.

Tristan: Hey, can you call me when you're free?

I dialed his number immediately. Tristan and I had been in regular contact, but the big brother in me couldn't help worrying about him.

"Hey, is everything okay?" I asked.

"Yeah," he laughed. "You didn't need to call straight away. You must be busy."

"Nah, not for you. What's up?"

"Ben's favorite author, A. Lawton, is signing at a con in Vegas next month. I want to take him, and since it's Vegas, I wondered what you think about making it my bachelor's trip."

"Man, are you fucking serious? Sign me up with bells on. Who else is coming?"

"So far, Wren and Tom. I think Indy is checking if Jake can cover for him."

"Anything I can do to help?"

"Just turn up with your sunny disposition."

I laughed out loud. "Tell me when. I'll be there, Kiddo."

We finished the call, and I looked at the clock. Fuck, I had five minutes.

I dashed to the office kitchen while I dialed Indy's number. Some kind of angel had made coffee recently, so I just had to pick a cup and fill it.

"You sound excited. You're at work...right?" Indy said as soon as he picked up the call.

"Yes. There's fresh coffee, and I have a meeting in five. These days, this is reason enough to throw a party."

"No cinnamon buns?"

I groaned. "My local bakery was all out this morning. Life's so not fair."

"Poor Tate, going without his heavenly scented sugary treats."

"I hate you."

"Nah, you love me. Now tell me how can I help because my piping bag just split in my hand and there's cream everywhere."

I coughed the sip of coffee I'd just taken, and my dick hardened in my slacks.

"Fuck, Indy."

"What? It's the—"

"Buttercream, yes, you said." I cleared my throat before I continued. "Tristan just called about Vegas."

"Yeah, he was here earlier. It's awesome, right? I've never been to Vegas. Fuck, I haven't had a vacation in so long I don't even know where my swimming trunks are," he said.

Images of Indy skinny dipping came to mind. And my semi was officially full hard-on.

"So you're coming?" I asked.

"Yeah, Jake can cover, and the part-timer said she'd help out. It's only a long weekend, I don't think the good people of Chester Falls will die if I run out of buns."

"You clearly never had your buns," I teased.

"Tate!"

"I'm saying this in a one hundred percent friendly capaci-ty...I'd lick your buns from top to bottom every day if I could."

He sighed.

"You promised no flirting. We're friends."

Thank you for the reminder. Whose fucking idea was it, anyway? Oh yeah, this fucking idiot with the chubby at work.

"You make it too easy. Besides, you were the one who started it."

"I fail to see how."

"You mentioned cream all over you," I said.

"You're a terrible attorney. I mentioned *butter*cream everywhere."

"Well I heard cream, and by cream I mean—"

"Bye, Tate."

I laughed. "Speak later, Tightbuns."

I put my phone inside my drawer as a knock on the open door of my office caught my attention.

"You better clean that smooshy smile off your face. You're meeting your new about-to-be-divorced client," Harrison said. "It's not good form when the attorney is smiling like the cat that got the cream when he comes in."

"Got it, boss."

He shook his head.

"Hey, Hare..."

"What."

"Tristan's bachelor trip is next month. Will you pick up my load if I need a couple days off?"

"Sure, in exchange for all the sordid details. I want you to leave nothing out."

"Got it."

"*A*re you sure you don't want to wait upstairs with us?" Ben asked.

"Yeah, I'm sure. He should be here soon."

The truth was that I was feeling too antsy to be around anyone. I hadn't seen Tate in over two months, so I was nervous as hell, which made no sense because we talked to each other every day, if not by call or video call, at least by message.

"If you're sure you don't want any company, then Wren is going to check out our suite, and I'm going to check out Wren," Tom said, looking unabashedly at Wren, who looked like he was very much up for being checked out.

"I'm sure. I guess I'll see you all in a couple of hours by the pool?" I said.

Tom made a face as if he was mentally adding up how long he needed for what he had in mind, and Ben pushed his glasses up on his nose and looked adoringly at Tristan.

"God, you four make me sick," I joked. "I'll go to the pool when Tate gets here, and you come down when you're ready."

All our suitcases had already been sent up to each of the

suites, so I sat down on the comfortable looking couches by the check-in desk.

My phone buzzed with a message.

Tate: In the taxi, nearly there.
Indy: Not soon enough. The lovebirds have already disappeared into their nests.
Tate: Hope Tom booked us into something bigger than a nest. With how much money we paid, it better have a butler and a chef.
Indy: It'll definitely have a baker ;)
Tate: It's the best suite ever, already :D

I pocketed my phone, deciding to do some people watching while I waited for Tate, but a beautiful display of pastries caught my attention, and the baker in me couldn't resist.

The prices were atrocious, but looking was free, so I marveled at the beautifully crafted cream-filled pastries, perfectly symmetrical macarons, and the scent emanating from the area. I could get high on that alone.

"I should have known I'd find you within a few feet of cake."

I turned around and jumped into Tate's arms, only just short of wrapping my legs around him.

"Oh shit, sorry, I shouldn't have done that," I said, trying to pull back.

He tightened his hold and inhaled. "Hmm, I missed your smell, Tightbuns."

"I missed you, too," I said.

We both stood back looking at each other, checking if we were still the same people. Tate had filled out a little more. I didn't think it was possible, but it seemed it was because he was all six and a half feet of hard muscle, sexy beard, and captivating eyes.

"Um, shall we go check up our suite? The guys are meeting at the pool later."

"Sounds good. I could do with getting out of these clothes."

I gave him one of the key cards, and we headed for the elevator.

"Did you have a good flight?" I asked.

"Yeah, shame I couldn't get a direct one like yours. Sorry for being late."

"That's okay."

Nothing would have prepared me for the opulence of the suite. We dropped Tate's suitcase next to mine by the door in the hallway with the marble floor. Yes, the suite had a hallway...and a marble floor.

I looked at Tate, who was as shocked as I was.

"I guess this explains the price tag," he said.

We followed the hall into a large living area that had a couch big enough for a small crowd, a kitchen that was better equipped than the small one I had in my apartment, and a balcony with a view of the fountains.

"I'm never leaving," I said, looking at the view. I bet it was even better at nighttime.

"And you haven't seen the rooms yet," Tate said from the door to one of the rooms.

"Oh, where's my room?" There wasn't another door next to Tate's room. I walked around the suite, but all the doors led to cupboards, a bathroom with a jacuzzi bath, and the balcony.

"Indy, there isn't another room," Tate said.

"How? We booked a two bed suite, let me call the reception desk."

I tapped my fingers nervously on my knees as I waited for the call to be answered.

"Hello, reception. This is Brandy, how may I help?"

"Hi Brandy, my name is Indigo Birch, and I'm in Suite

1067. I believe we've been given the wrong suite. We booked a two bedroom suite. Can you please check?"

"Certainly, Sir. One moment."

Tate sat next to me and covered my hand with his.

"I'm really sorry, sir, but there's no reservation under that name."

"Oh god, I'm sorry, I should have given you my friend's name. He was the one that placed the booking. Thomas Angel Jones."

I heard the tap-tap of computer keys on the other side of the phone.

"Sir, I'm afraid the booking was for three, one-bedroom suites. It's a bachelor party, right?"

"Yes. Um, Brandy...how much would it cost to change it?"

"It would be an additional three thousand dollars, Sir, but due to the literary conference we're hosting this weekend, we don't have any other available suites."

"Okay, um, thank you."

"You're welcome, sir. Would that be all?"

"Yes."

"Enjoy your stay with us."

I put the phone down on its cradle and faced Tate.

"There are no more rooms."

He frowned. "But didn't Tom..."

"No, looks like this is what he booked."

I stood up and looked around. This was a big, fancy room, right? I bet the couch had a bed in it.

"Get up," I asked.

"What?"

"Get up. This may be a convertible couch."

I started pulling all the cushions off to find something to pull or a button to press.

"Indy."

"Wait, hold on, I think I got it."

"Indy..."

"What?" I said, releasing my arm from under the couch.

"We can sleep in the same bed. Come into the room. The bed is definitely big enough."

"But...um..." My skin felt too hot. Wasn't there air conditioning in this room?

"Indy," Tate said, coming over and putting a hand on either of my shoulders. "We've slept together before. We can share. Do you trust me?"

I nodded. The problem wasn't that I didn't trust Tate when it came to it. The problem was that I didn't trust myself. Just being around Tate had my hairs standing up, my dick constantly hard, and looking at him made me want to burrow in his chest.

"I'm not responsible for any cuddling that may happen while I'm sleeping," I mumbled.

"We'll build a pillow fort if we need to. Now, shall we get changed and go down to the pool?"

"Okay, let's do it."

I was glad we both agreed to change in the bathroom...separately, because I didn't need to see naked Tate. Nope. No matter how much I really wanted it, because people normally didn't see their friends naked, and he was my friend.

Surprisingly, the guys were all by the pool when we finally made it outside.

"I'm not sure I'm impressed or disappointed that you're all here already," I laughed.

Tate went to get us some drinks, so I took the opportunity to pull Tom aside.

"Did you know you booked us a one-bedroom suite?" I asked in a low voice.

Tom looked at Wren who gave him a look and then turned to speak to Tristan.

"Um...really? I must have made a mistake... Sorry?" he said, shrugging his shoulders and not looking sorry at all.

"We want different things, Tom. In fact, the only thing we

can agree on is that we want each other, but that doesn't take us very far when one of us doesn't believe in relationships," I said.

"My muse said once 'Since everything is in our heads, we had better not lose them,' but I think in your and Tate's case, it would do you good to lose your heads just one time. They don't say what happens in Vegas stays in Vegas for nothing, my friend."

It was easier said than done, especially when he'd already found the love of his life.

I thought I'd found him once, but since then I'd met guys that had made me feel so much more than my ex ever had, and sadly, Tate was one of those men. Maybe even the top spot holder, but he didn't want the prize. He didn't even want to be in the competition.

With my track record, how would I even identify the guy that would be the one? There were so many factors to consider. It made my head hurt.

Should I just have some fun this weekend? Put all the responsibilities behind me for a few days.

Maybe I'd consider Tom's words later once I had a few drinks in me. Now? I just wanted to go for a refreshing dip in the pool, followed by a cool drink.

TATE

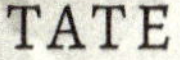

When I came back from the bar, Indy was in the pool and the happy couples were chatting about wedding stuff. I sat on my deck chair intent on ignoring them and focused instead on drinking my cocktail and watching Indy.

His bun was a wet mess on his head, but somehow he'd never looked more beautiful. It looked like he'd been exercising since I'd last seen him because his slim but soft body now had some definition. He hadn't mentioned anything to me before.

Even from a distance, I followed the droplets of water cascading from his hair and down the new lines of his back muscles.

I had to force myself to look away because ever since I'd seen Indy salivating over the pastries earlier, I'd wanted nothing but to buy a box and feed them to him in bed.

Fuck.

I had to sit up and grab a spare towel to place over my shorts to hide my erection. Whose idea was it to come to the pool?

At least the drink was nice and refreshing, if a little more alcoholic than I expected considering the amount of syrup I'd seen the bartender pour on it.

I looked at Indy again. My hand tightened on the glass when I saw him chatting to a guy in the pool. They were both laughing and then he pointed our way and waved. Everyone waved back but me. I was busy holding a drink...and the towel over my shorts.

Indy and the guy turned back toward the other swimmers and the pool and continued their conversation. The guy put his hand on Indy's shoulder and said something closer to his ear.

What the fuck?

Indy nodded and they both laughed. He didn't even refuse the guy's contact.

"Calm down, big boy," Tom said in a low voice, placing his hand on my arm. I hadn't even realized I was sitting straighter in my chair. "He's single and maybe he's ready to mingle...isn't he?"

I huffed and sat back on the chair. I had no reason to be jealous. After all, we were just friends on mutual agreement, but fuck if my hackles didn't rise at the thought of Indy staying the night in another guy's room so he wouldn't have to share with me.

Or maybe that was a good thing since it solved our problem.

"That guy is freakin' hilarious. He's here with his grand-parents who are on their constellation anniversary - his words, not mine. They've been married for so long they've outgrown all the precious stones. I hope you don't mind, but I said he could maybe look us up after dinner once his grandparents go to their room."

I didn't know where Indy had suddenly appeared from, but dripping wet with a big relaxed smile on his face was a look that suited him.

He pulled my towel and sat sideways at *my* feet on *my* deck chair, drying off and then retying his hair.

"Oh, is that drink for me?" he asked, pointing at the small table next to me.

I passed him the tall glass and lost a breath when he smiled and wrapped his lips around the straw to take a sip.

Does he know what he's doing to me?

He winked and then turned to the guys.

"So what were you talking about?" he asked, leaning back a little on the chair and using one hand as support. I pulled my knees further into my chest, which was the most ridiculous position to be for a guy of my height and size.

All I'd need now to complete my utter embarrassment was for the chair to break, which would happen at the same time as my swimming trunks would give in and tear like wet paper to show everyone what an Indy-induced erection looked like.

"Vegas wedding," Wren said. "I guess I expected a little less luxury. I'd totally get married here."

Tom gasped and took Wren's cocktail away from his hand.

"No more juice for you. Imagine telling our children we got married in Vegas. Do you think they'd imagine this opulence? No, they'd think we did it because you knocked me up and felt responsible."

I snorted.

Wren pulled Tom to his deck chair, proving they were actually stronger than they looked, and wrapped his arms around him.

"Baby..." He drawled. "We'll get married wherever you want, and not just because I knocked you up. Although we could practice some later in our suite."

Tom relaxed in Wren's embrace and sighed.

"I don't see the problem. Get it over with quickly and save the money for the honeymoon," I said.

Five pairs of eyes looked my way.

"What? It's not that big of a deal. Everyone professes their undying love until they step into my office ready to tear each other to shreds."

There were a lot of looks exchanged between them, but Indy was the only one that spoke. "Regardless of how a marriage ends, when it starts, it's a special day in a couple's journey together, and most people want to share it with their family."

"Not everyone," I said, getting up. "I'm going to take a nap. I'll meet you later for dinner."

What I needed was a cold shower to reset whatever was twisting me in more knots than a cable sweater.

The door to the bathroom slammed open.

"What the hell was that?" Indy asked.

"What was what?" I replied, turning the shower on and only then around to face him. He was definitely angry.

"Your little speech."

"Everything I said was the truth," I said, pushing my trunks to the floor and walking into the shower. The barely warm water was perfect.

"So it's okay to hurt your brother, his fiancé, and our friends just to make a point."

His voice sounded closer, so I moved my head from under the spray and opened my eyes.

"Are you so jaded by what happened to you that you honestly believe no one will ever be happy? Well, I can tell you *my* parents defy your beliefs." He came even closer, his finger pointing at me. "*My* parents love each other like no one else I've ever seen. Tom and Wren are the real deal. Tristan and Ben, too."

My cock was so hard from Indy's passionate argument, and it was a surprise he hadn't noticed it. He was so close now, the spray from the shower was getting to him. "If you stopped just for a second and looked, *really looked*, at how they are around each other, you'd just know that their kind of love is forever. And maybe it won't happen to all of us, but—"

I couldn't take it any longer. I pulled Indy to me and slammed my lips onto his.

Even with his swimming trunks on, I felt his dick harden as I plunged into his mouth. I was starved for his taste, and now that I'd broken the seal on the jar, all my need was spilling out.

"God, you drive me crazy," I said, sucking on his bottom lip.

Indy's hands explored my chest, moving down until he got hold of my dick and gave it a long hard stroke.

"You're a dick, you know that?" he said, pushing me so my back was against the wall.

He went on his knees and took my cock in his mouth, sucking the crown before taking it all the way until the head touched his throat. He hummed and hollowed his cheeks, sucking so hard I thought my brain was going to leave me through my dick. There was a strong possibility it already had.

"Come here," I said, pulling him up to his feet to kiss him. I was too close to coming, and if I only had this one chance with Indy, I wanted to make it count.

"This doesn't mean we're going to be more than friends," he said, even as his hands stroked my face and then tugged on my short hair to keep me from moving.

"Uh huh," I moaned into his mouth.

"And it doesn't mean we're doing this again."

"Yeah..."

I grabbed his hands and turned us around so he was the one against the tiles, and then turned him so I was face to face with his perfect, tight ass.

"And you're...oh fuck," he shouted as I used my hands to separate his cheeks and licked a path from his balls to his hole. He pushed back onto my face.

He tasted of chlorine, vanilla, and man. If he choked me to death with his ass, I'd die happy. I might actually consider adding that to my medical papers.

In case of impending death, smother with Indy's ass for compassionate release from this world.

I chuckled.

"I didn't realize my ass was funny," he said.

"Your ass is perky, tight, and delicious, baby, and I'm going to feast on it until you're screaming my name and coming gloriously on these tiles."

"Do it," he demanded breathlessly.

I didn't know what possessed me to chase after Tate, but finding myself against a shower wall while he ate my ass was not the outcome I'd expected.

Still, beggars couldn't be choosers, and the way Tate was teasing my hole with his tongue and sucking around it had me begging like I had never fucking begged before.

"Fuck, Tightbuns, you taste like the best dessert in the world," Tate said.

"Shut up and don't stop," I gritted.

I was already naked and on the verge of a phenomenal orgasm. I could handle him owning my body. I could handle him pushing me to the edge of heaven and never quite letting me cross the gates.

But, I couldn't handle him saying all the things that made me feel like we were something to each other. More than friends. Intimate. Lovers.

Movement from the corner of my eye caught my attention. For a moment, I stilled and Tate stopped. He looked at me and followed my line of sight.

Our eyes met in the floor to ceiling mirror I'd missed

earlier. There was hardly any steam in the bathroom, so I had a perfect view. I swallowed as I surveyed our reflection.

Tate was on his knees behind me, both his hands on the globes on my ass, keeping my cheeks apart so he could taste me. His cock was hard, and because the water from the shower sprayed on my back and then his, I could see the beads of precum leaking from him.

"Touch yourself," I commanded.

He didn't move his gaze from mine as he released one of his hands from my ass to grip his cock. He gave it a long, slow stroke, his eyelids closing as he twisted his wrist slightly.

"I want you to make me come with you," I commanded.

Who the hell was this horny, bossy person I saw in the mirror? I didn't care as long as it got me what I'd craved for the last two months. One more orgasm at Tate's hands, or in this case, mouth.

"I'm close, baby," he said.

I wanted to tell him to stop with the endearments because it made me die a little inside every time I heard them when there was no meaning behind them, but my words became stuck in my throat. I was only breathing the essential amount needed for me to survive this ordeal.

Tate's tongue plunged inside me, fucking me like it could reach the depths of my soul. His beard rasped against my skin, heightening all the sensations.

I closed my eyes and let the fireball of pleasure erupt from the core of my body, destroying every cell that was Indy on its path, and mutating them into a form of messy, but satisfied, goo.

"Tate!" I shouted my orgasm. My legs threatened to give out. I looked at the mirror again and saw ropes of cum jetting out of Tate's cock. My dick jerked as if it could go for another round at the sight of him with his face still in my ass and his mouth near a very distinct bite mark. When did that happen?

He sat down and pulled me to straddle him, turning the shower off.

"Don't go out with him," he said, tracing small patterns on my chest with his fingers.

"With who?"

"The guy from the pool."

I put my hands on his. "You know you can't ask me that, Tate."

He sighed. "I know."

"Why aren't we doing this, Tate?"

"Doing what?"

I ran my hands over his arms. With the almost cold shower water, his skin was full of goosebumps. "Me...you."

"Because we want different things."

That was true initially, but when was the last time I'd been with someone with the intention of pursuing more than a one night stand? When was the last time I'd given anyone a chance?

Maybe I was more like Tate than I thought.

"What if we don't?"

"What do you mean?" he asked, his eyes roaming my face looking for answers.

"What if we want the same things, Tate? Do you want to be with anyone else?"

"No." He shook his head. "I haven't wanted anyone since...three months ago when I last used my hookup app and met a sassy, sexy baker with an intriguing name and even more intriguing personality. Let's not even mention his buns."

I laughed and gave him a quick kiss but pulled back when he tried to deepen it.

"I don't want anyone else, either, and I'm tired of pretending I don't want you."

"Indy, I need you to know my opinion on relationships or marriage won't change. We can't go into this if you think you can change me."

His words didn't hurt me as I thought they would. After all, he was being honest with me and himself.

"We have fundamentally different beliefs about relationships, I know that, but our reality isn't so different from each other. That night at the bar wasn't the first time I used that app or gone there with the intention of finding someone," I said.

Tate gasped. "Are you saying you weren't a virgin on our first time together?"

I tried to hit him on his shoulder but he caught my hand and maneuvered us so I was suddenly on the hard tiled floor of the shower.

"So, we're doing this..." he said, running his nose up my neck.

"Uh huh."

"Am I going to be your dirty little secret?"

My dick started hardening again.

"Fuck, Tate," I breathed out.

"Oh, you like that idea, do you?"

It was fucked up, but I did like the idea of keeping him just to myself. I also didn't want to face any judgment from the happy couples. Not everyone got to meet their soulmate, but I was lucky enough that at least there was plenty of chemistry between Tate and me.

He kissed my chest, and tugged on my barbell, moving down slowly until he reached my cock, but instead of taking it in his mouth, he kissed my hip and said, "Shall we take this up to the bedroom?"

"Yes please, with a proper cherry on top. Not the glacé ones. Those are gross."

He shook his head. "Oh, Indy, what am I going to do with you?"

"I'm sure you'll think of something. Now, why don't you use your big muscles to carry me to bed? And please tell me you have condoms."

"Indy, baby, I have condoms."

We didn't leave the bedroom until it was time to meet the others for dinner.

As soon as we stepped into the elevator, I panicked thinking they'd know what we'd been up to all afternoon. Especially because even the shower, on my own this time, hadn't done anything to make the blush in my face disappear or reduce the swelling on my lips.

"I look like I've been fucked within an inch of my life," I groaned, staring at the mirror.

"I'm not sorry about that," Tate said.

"Don't look so smug. We agreed we'd keep this between us."

He raised his hands up and I walked into him, my heart skipping a tiny beat as he wrapped his arms around me. We broke apart just before the doors to the elevator opened on the restaurant level.

The guys were lining up to get into the restaurant so we joined them.

"Where's Wren?" I asked.

"His best friend is here this weekend, so he was going to check if he can join us," Tristan said. I noticed he exchanged a discreet look with Tom. What was that about?

"Before we go in, can I say something?" Tate asked. He looked at me and then at Tristan, Ben, and Tom. "I'm sorry about earlier. I have...beliefs about relationships. Those are my issues, and I shouldn't have talked about weddings like I did. I want to blame my job as a divorce attorney, but I was already a jerk before that."

Tristan gave Tate a hug and said there were no hard feelings. I couldn't help feeling a little bit of relief on Tate's behalf. From what Tate had told me, they were rebuilding their relationship and he didn't want to mess it up. Another reason we couldn't tell anyone about us.

We were going through the drinks list when Wren arrived

with a guy that looked like he was out of a Ralph Lauren ad. Blond, blue eyes, clean-cut, and dressed in clothes I was sure only Tom would identify as designer.

Ben gasped and went beet red.

"Everyone, this is my friend Aiden, from San Diego. Here's here for the author conference Ben is attending tomorrow."

"Nice to meet you, Aiden," I said as he took one of the empty seats at the table. "Are you hoping to meet your favorite authors like Ben is?"

Tate coughed and straightened up in his chair, using the move to place his hand on my leg under the table.

Smooth bastard.

I leaned forward and laced my fingers with his under the table.

"No," Aiden said. "I'm actually signing tomorrow."

"Oh, you're an author. That's awesome. Ben owns the best bookstore ever, and he's started writing, too, but he won't share any of his work, even when I try to bribe him with cinnamon buns." I looked at Ben who was trying to hide behind Tristan.

I tried to make sense of all the covert exchanges between everyone, but there was no point. My whole body was tuned into Tate's circular motion of his thumb on my palm.

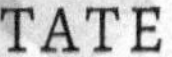

No, I wasn't jealous. Okay, Aiden wasn't just gorgeous, he also seemed like a nice guy, but I was touching Indy because I wanted to and because I could, and because he was mine.

Okay, I was totally jealous that Aiden seemed to be some kind of guest of honor and Indy was fascinated by the fact he was an author.

"So, Ben," Aiden said. "Who's your favorite author? Who are you hoping to meet tomorrow?"

Ben shrunk into himself. He looked adorably star struck.

"Um...A. Lawton, I mean...um...you," he said.

Aiden smiled and looked at Wren.

It was at this point that Tristan confessed that this trip had been an engagement present to Ben after Tristan and Wren figured out that Ben's favorite author was, in fact, Wren's best friend.

Since Wren and Aiden hadn't seen each other for months, they thought it was a good opportunity to catch up and for Ben to meet Aiden outside of the confusion of the conference.

The food was great and the guys were fun, but throughout

dinner, Indy had teased me senseless by running his hand up and down my leg under the table.

"If you don't stop that, I'm going to have to drag you under the table and have you for dessert," I said as quietly as I could.

Indy pretended he didn't hear me, but his hand tightened ever so slightly on my leg and his fingers brushed against my hard-on. I'd have thought that two more rounds of sex after the first one in the shower would have my dick begging for mercy, but no, the horny bastard couldn't get enough of Indy.

"Okay, guys, who's up for shaking what yo momma gave ya on the dance floor?" Indy asked. "I need to work off this dinner."

Aiden raised both hands and said, "Sorry, early night for me. Besides, I need to check in on my boyfriend. He always gets stressed out before events."

"I thought you'd be the one who'd get stressed," I said.

Aiden took a deep breath and looked at Wren. "Richard is also my agent, so he'll spend the day tomorrow schmoozing people."

I could tell there was more to it, but I didn't care enough to ask.

Both Tristan and Ben, and Wren and Tom said they wanted an early night, too.

Indy turned to me with a teasing look. "What do you say, Big Boy? Do you want to show me your moves on the dance floor?"

Tristan laughed. "Tate? Dancing? When we were kids, our parents enrolled us in ballroom dancing. Don't ask. Tate got kicked out in the first week."

"Why?" Indy asked.

I felt my face warm up even though it had been twenty years since the event, and as long since I'd thought about it.

"Because they made me dance with a girl and I refused," I said. "Mr. I'm-a-good-boy over there should have taken a stand with me but bailed out to dance with a girl." I pretended to shudder.

"Mr. I'm-a-good-boy likes good boys these days, even when he's feeling like being not so good," Tristan said.

"TMI, Bro, TMI."

I got up and put my hand out to Indy, "Come on, Sweet Buns, let's go show these old farts how the single dudes do it."

A crowd of woos followed, so Indy stuck his tongue out and took my hand.

There were already a few people on the dance floor. I raised Indy's hand to force a twirl and then caught him when he turned back to me. He put both his hands on my chest and wrapped my arms around his waist.

"I hope you know I was totally bluffing out there," I said. "I haven't got a dancing bone in my body."

"Well, I wouldn't say that." He winked and pressed closer to me.

"Indy..."

He chuckled. "Don't worry, if you move fast enough no one will see you."

"If I move fast enough, I'll break my neck, yours, and possibly everyone else's around us."

The music went from a soft beat to a slow one, so we carried on swaying from side to side.

"I really want to kiss you right now," I said.

Indy bit his lip and looked at me like he wouldn't object to it, but I knew there was a one hundred percent chance the guys were still looking our way.

"Don't give me that look. You're gonna kill my dick if we don't give it a break."

"You think my ass isn't sore? Your dick should come with a health warning."

"I warned you after the first time," I said.

"So you did, but my ass was too horny to listen."

"We've got to stop talking about sex or those old ladies

over there are going to see more than they paid for in this show."

Indy looked at the ladies and winked. The old hussies winked right back at him. I just shook my head.

"I have an idea," I said, pulling him by the hand toward our table where the only ones left were Tom and Wren.

"You guys sure you don't want to come out?" I asked.

"Nope, Wren promised we were trying for a baby...or three tonight," Tom said.

Wren nodded and they both left us.

"I'd be jealous, but I'm so letting you tap my ass later," Indy said.

"Come on, I know where we can go."

If there was one best man thing I did well, it was researching LGBT bars in Vegas, and tonight I was up for trying a few with Indy.

We picked up a cab in front of the hotel, and within ten minutes, we were off the strip in a street lined with bars and clubs.

Freedrag was a mix between a bar and a nightclub. Their website had promised weekly drag shows on Fridays.

"Oh look," Indy said, pointing at a big billboard. "If you're engaged to be married in Vegas you get free entry. What do you say, wanna marry me for the sole purpose of getting in there for free?"

He didn't wait for my answer before he pulled me to the queue. It was slow-moving, so I placed him with his back to my chest and wrapped my arms around him.

"Do you think the guys will want to join us tomorrow?" I asked him. He turned his face and gave me a quick kiss.

"I hope so. This looks like a fun place."

The couple in front of us turned around.

"We've been here every night this week. It has such a great atmosphere, and it's very safe," one of the guys said. "Are you getting married, too?"

"Oh um..."

"Yes," Indy said. "We're so in love it's insane. Right babe?"

I chuckled and nodded.

"Aww, you're so cute together," the other guy said. "You should come to our wedding. It's tonight at the Rainbow Chapel. They do LGBT weddings. You should check it out for your wedding."

I hadn't drunk anything tonight, and here I was, standing in a queue pretending to be engaged to Indy and somehow agreeing to be a guest at a stranger's wedding.

"You're getting married tonight, and you're here?" Indy asked.

They both nodded with big smiles as if it made total sense.

Suddenly, I really liked those guys. Yes, they were probably doing the stupidest thing ever, but they were having fun. There was no guest list with hundreds of people. No expectations. Just them.

I tightened my arms around Indy and kissed the back of his neck. He shivered in my hold despite the warm night.

The club inside was hot and loud, but I had to give it to the DJ. The music was great. Between us and the other couple, I'd lost count of how many cocktails we'd drank after a couple of hours.

"Let's dance some more," Indy said. He pulled my hand and the hand of the other guy. His fiancé followed us so we ended up in a group all dancing together. "You know," he said, slurring his words, "if we keep drinking we won't get a hangover because we'll just be drunk."

I laughed, contemplating the argument. It kinda made sense, so to show my appreciation for his sexy brains, I kissed him until he was writhing against me.

"Fuck, Tate, you're so sexy I feel like I want to live inside you," he said. "No, that's not right. I want you to live inside me."

He looked at me. His face scrunched up and then he

smiled. "Yes, that's it. I want you to live inside me."

"You made me fall in love with romantic movies."

I don't know why I felt the need to tell him that, but I thought he should know, so I said it. What was the point of leaving things unsaid? After all, Indy was mine now because we both said we wanted to live inside each other. Or at least that's what I think we said. Either way, it ended up with very hot sex.

Indy's dance moves were slow and sensual as if he was making love to me in front of everyone else. It was hot and sexy and forbidden but still legal because we had clothes on. I checked in my legal brain. *Yup.*

We all left the club together, after who knew how long because I'd lost track of time, and jumped into a cab.

"I'm going to fuck you five ways into Sunday," I said.

The other guys laughed.

"Oh fuck, did I say that out loud?"

Six heads nodded. Who were the other two guys?

"Oh baby, I didn't know you had a twin," I said to Indy.

He didn't answer because he was too busy singing along with the music on the radio.

"This is our song, Tate. Who sings it? It's about lavender," he shouted with his hands raised up. "Lavender is our thing. Do you have a flower for your wedding?" he asked the guys.

I closed my eyes, listening to the song by Marillion and letting it drown the voices.

I heard the hum of the bees in the wind, saw the purple flowers, and Indy's blue hair floating all around us. His eyes were precious stones, and his smile was only for me.

When the song stopped, there was silence in the cab. The other guys were kissing.

I put my hands on Indy's face to make sure he listened to me because what I was going to say was important. What was I going to say? Oh yeah.

"Indy, I had the best idea ever."

INDY

"**W**hat's that noise?" I groaned, my voice sounding alien, even to me. Probably thanks to the sack of cotton balls someone had stuffed in my mouth.

"Don't know. Stop singing," Tate groaned back.

"I'm not singing."

I extended my hand in the general direction of the sound. My fingers touched my phone, and I pressed a button that seemed to have stopped it. *Result.*

Tate pulled me to him and nuzzled my neck.

God, it was nice not waking up alone.

"Why are there roadworks outside?" I asked.

"We're on the twentieth floor. There are no roads up here," he said.

"Then wh—"

"Shhh. Sleep, baby."

I turned over and found my favorite chest of all time, and then my favorite arms of all time wrapped around me, and then I heard that rumble in his chest that was my personal morning soundtrack.

My phone rang again. When had I changed the ringtone to Lavender by Marillion?

I opened one eye to locate my phone, and my eyeballs were stabbed by a million tiny pins.

Fuck, how much did I have to drink yesterday?

I swiped the screen to answer.

"Hello?"

"Hey, sleeping beauty," Tom said, far too chirpy for my liking. "Are you guys coming down for breakfast?"

I groaned my reply and heard Tom laughing.

"Indy? Is everything okay?" Ben asked, taking over the call.

"Tell them to go away. This is my time," Tate said, sounding like he wasn't feeling any better than I was.

"Tate? Indy, why is Tate—"

"We'll be down in ten," I said, ending the call. "Come on, Tree Man. Let's meet them for breakfast."

"If I smell any food, I might get sick."

"We'll just have coffee and then come up for a nap. Come on."

He groaned but relented.

I felt a tiny bit more human once I washed my face and brushed my teeth. Tate, too, if the state of his morning wood was any kind of measure.

"Stop staring at it or I'll bend you over the sink and fuck you right now," he said with the toothbrush still in his mouth.

I got in front of him and gave his erection a slow tug. "Coffee first."

He leaned over the sink to rinse his mouth. "Look in the dictionary for the definition of 'tease,' and you'll find your name there, Indigo Birch. You know what happens to teases like you?"

"They get a nice dicking after breakfast?"

This time, it was Tate's turn to push us to get dressed and out the door.

"Jesus, you two look like death," Ben said as we approached the table.

"Don't worry, we feel like it, too," I said. "Are you excited about today?"

He smiled wide and nodded. "I can't believe I got to meet A. Lawton last night. Did you know he's been to Chester Falls to visit Wren and Tom, and I never bumped into him? Aiden promised to come by Bookmarked next time he's there so we can talk about writing."

Tate came back to the table with two cups of the darkest coffee and two cinnamon buns.

He shrugged. "I'm already preparing myself for the disappointment, but cinnamon is the only smell I can tolerate right now."

I picked one up and took a bite. They were delicious. Between the buns and the coffee, I could feel my energy levels increasing already.

After breakfast, Tom and Wren said they were going to check out the designer stores, so with Tristan and Ben at the conference, Tate and I decided to take a nap and then go to the pool later.

"I hope you realize I didn't really mean a *nap* nap, right?" Tate said, pulling me closer in the elevator and giving me a coffee and cinnamon-flavored kiss.

"I hope you realize I was counting on it not being a nap."

We stumbled into the suite, hands and mouths everywhere, hangover still a slight annoyance, but I was too horny to care.

"Wait, let me put the keycard on the table. I don't want to spend an hour looking for it later," Tate said.

I nodded but didn't stop touching him.

"What's this?" he asked.

"What's what?"

Tate had a sheet of paper in his hand, and it looked like there was a photo of us on the table, too.

He looked at me, his eyes wide and panicked.

"What's wrong?"

"This is a wedding certificate," he said.

"What?"

I took the paper from his hands. It was a marriage certificate with both our names on it.

"No, this must be wrong. Didn't we agree to be witnesses to those other two guys? What were their names again?"

"I don't fucking care what their names were, Indy. This is a marriage certificate, and it has both our names as the groom and groom."

I picked up the photo from the table. Underneath, there were two wedding bands. I ignored them and looked at the photo. There we were, holding our hands up with the rings on our wedding fingers. Tate was looking at me like he finally found what he'd been looking for all his life.

A frog lodged itself in my throat, and I had to put the photo down. I picked up the rings. They were simple gold bands. No inscriptions.

Tate walked to the large window overlooking the fountains. He had his hands in his hair like he wanted to tear it out. The playfulness from earlier was completely gone and all there was left was tension.

"Hold on," I said. "Let's think about this. We'd need a marriage license in order to get married, right?" He nodded. "God, Tate. We were too drunk last night to fill any kind of official paperwork, let alone actually get married." He nodded again. "Besides, do you think *you* of all people would do it? I mean, this is Vegas, but you're so against marriage, I doubt even drunk, you would have allowed yourself to go ahead with it."

He turned around and came back to me. His eyes were scared, haunted. He put his hands on my face and stared right into me. "I can't do this to you, Indy. Not you. I can't..." And then he kissed me.

"Tate," I said into his lips before I put some space between us. "Why don't we go to the chapel and check this out?"

I picked up the photo, rings, and certificate while Tate picked up the keys, and we left.

"Hey, it's the lavender grooms," the cab driver said as we got in the car.

"You know us?" I asked.

"Of course. It's been a long night, and you're my last trip before I go home to my wife, but I remember you two love birds."

Tate and I looked at each other.

"Where did you drop us off?" Tate asked.

"Let me see, after you proposed, your friends helped you fill in the Licence Pre-Application online on your phone and then I dropped you off at the Marriage Licence Bureau, so you could pick the licence up," the cab driver said.

"I...um...proposed?" Tate looked at me. A vague memory came to me, but I didn't dare voice it.

Indy...my beautiful, interesting, intriguing Indy. You must have baked a spell into your cinnamon buns because since that first night, I haven't been able to live without you constantly in my thoughts. I lost a client last month because I convinced them to give their marriage another chance. I don't know what you're doing to me, but I want more of it, and I want it now and forever. Please marry me.

He had proposed.

I looked away toward the street outside the cab as a small tear ran down my cheek. I cleaned it discreetly.

However Tate had felt last night, it was obviously a by-product of too much alcohol. It didn't matter, anyway, because we just needed to find out if the marriage certificate was legal and then figure out how to handle it.

The cab driver dropped us off at the chapel and left us with congratulations and wishes for a long, happy life. Whoever his wife was, she was a lucky woman.

I stared at the chapel. It had a giant rainbow right above the front door and a rainbow carpet leading inside. I laughed.

If this wedding was real, then I'd finally fulfilled one of my dreams, the biggest one, and I had no recollection of any of it.

"What are you laughing at? Did you remember something?" Tate asked.

"No, nothing. Let's go in."

There was a slim woman behind a glass-fronted desk. She was dressed like a fifties pin-up girl. Her hair was a bright rainbow, and she had a smile to match.

"Hello there. Are you looking to get married today?" she asked.

"No, we um...think we got married here last night," I said and gave her the marriage certificate.

She looked at it and then started typing on her computer.

"Oh yes, I found it. This is a copy. We issue it because couples normally want to have a copy straight away, but that one isn't valid."

Tate leaned closer to the glass. "What does that mean, exactly?"

"It means your real license has been sent to be filed with the Clark County Recorder's Office. They will file it on Monday, which is when you'll be legally married. You'll get your marriage certificate in the mail within a few days."

"That's great," Tate said, sounding hopeful. "How can we stop it?"

She looked at him and me. "Stop what?"

"The marriage, um the certificate from being filed officially."

"Oh, honey, you can't. It's gone now."

Tate looked like all blood drained from his body at the same time. We slowly made our way outside.

I saw a cab nearby and called it.

"Come on. Let's go back to the hotel. We can figure things out when we get in."

He nodded and followed me to the cab.

No words were exchanged during the short drive to the

hotel. It was as if Tate was slipping away from me and I couldn't hold him back.

On our way up to the suite, we met Ben, who looked worried.

"Hey, is everything okay? Where's Tristan?"

"He's in the bathroom. We were going to grab lunch before going back to the conference. I just had a call from the company that was going to do the flowers for the wedding. They double booked and have to cancel on us."

I had two distressed men in front of me, but thankfully, one was easy to help.

"Tate, I'll meet you up in the suite," I said and then turned to Ben. "Let's get you the best flowers for your wedding. After all, I'm not your best man for nothing, right?"

A phone call to Reed later and Ben had what he needed and more. Reed had agreed to supply lavender arrangements at cost. I knew he'd been wondering about tapping the wedding market, but he was too worried that supplying lavender would impact on his crops.

Once that was sorted, I sent a much relieved Ben out to enjoy his lunch and the rest of the conference with Tristan and made my way upstairs.

When I opened the door to the suite, Tate was in the hallway with his suitcase packed.

My stomach sank. He was running, again.

"I'm sorry, Indy, I have to go back to Boston. We'll sort out this wedding mess. I can file for an annulment as soon as we get the certificate. My best friend has just called me. My goddaughter Megan was in an accident and she's in the hospital."

"Do you want me to go with you?"

"No, that's okay, thanks. I just need to make sure Harrison isn't on his own in the hospital while she's in surgery. Enjoy the rest of your weekend and apologize to the guys for me."

He gave me a kiss on the cheek and left.

TATE

"Hare," I said, running to my friend and wrapping him up in my arms. "How is she? How's Stella?"

"She's just gone into surgery. Fuck, Tate. I can't handle this."

I guided us to the sofa in the waiting room. "What happened?"

"Drunk driver. Came out of nowhere. Stella took the brunt of it, but they flipped over, so they had to be rescued out from under the car. Surprisingly, Stella's okay. She has a fractured leg and arm, and a few ribs but she's okay. Megan also has a broken leg, but hers requires surgery so the bone heals in place. The doctor said she may need further surgeries as she grows up, but they can't tell for sure at this stage."

"She'll be okay, Hare. They'll both be okay." I tried to reassure him even though I was fucking scared. I'd been there when Harrison and Stella got pregnant. I'd celebrated with them, visited Stella in the hospital as soon as Megan was born, and I'd fallen in love with the cute little baby with the big mop of brown hair and big brown eyes as soon as I'd laid my eyes on her.

I often joked with Harrison about not wanting kids, but

the truth was that to me, Megan was my kid, too, and I didn't need anyone else.

Harrison sighed. "Okay, we have a long wait ahead of us, and I don't want to be here thinking about my baby out there being cut up and pinned back together. Tell me about Vegas."

I groaned and ran my hands through my face and my beard.

"Would you believe me if I told you I got married?"

Harrison laughed. "Okay, I know we've got long to wait here, but there's no need to make up stories."

I looked at him.

"Oh fuck, you're not lying."

I shook my head.

"How did that happen?

"I wish I knew, but all I can tell you is that last night, I went dancing with Indy, we pretended to be engaged to get into a bar for free, then we met this fun couple, lot's of drinks, and woke up this morning married."

"So you don't actually remember anything."

"No."

I'd spent the entire flight out of Vegas poking in the depths of my memory for clues about last night, and there was very little to go on.

"We had an almost fight yesterday. We made up and ended up in bed. God, Hare, the electricity between us could power entire cities. It's *that* good."

"Hmm, now that's the kind of detail I want...carry on," he said, gesturing for me to continue.

"Pervert. So we decided to stop fighting this thing between us. We want different things from a relationship. Hell, I don't want a relationship at all."

"Liar, but carry on."

I gave him a pointed look. "Anyway, it was a mutual decision. It was so much fun flirting with him, and we teased each other over dinner knowing none of the other guys could know about us. It was fun, sexy, forbidden."

"Wait a minute. Tate, what the fuck are you doing here?" he asked.

"What do you mean? Megan and Stella were in an accident. Of course I have to be here."

"Shit, Tate. You should have told me. I'd never have asked you to come if I'd known."

I shook my head. "Hare, you're my family as much as my brother is, but he's happy with his fiancé having the bachelor trip of their dreams, and you're in the hospital waiting for your daughter to come out of surgery. There was no choice there."

He shifted on the sofa to face me. "You left him behind. If you were both in agreement about your relationship status, then he must be as confused as you are. And you left him there."

I stared at Harrison. *Fuck.*

"Can I ask you a question?"

"Sure," I said.

"Do yourself a favor and admit that you have feelings for him, Tate."

"That's not a question. Of course I have feelings for him. He's smart, funny, flirty, gorgeous, and has the biggest heart I've ever seen."

Being able to touch him freely when we were on our own yesterday was the best feeling ever. I wanted to always touch him, keep him close, kiss him whenever I wanted.

I looked into Harrison's brown eyes, who looked back at me with affection and understanding, as realization hit me.

"Hare, I've fallen in love with him."

"Of course you have, Tate. You're human, and despite what I normally tell you and what you believe about yourself, you're a good person. This is a wild guess because I don't know this guy, but I'd bet he's in love with you, too."

I shook my head. "No, he can't be. I'm going to hurt him." My chest hurt, and my eyes felt like they were burning.

"Tate, I've forgiven you. You know that, right?"

"I know, Hare, but it doesn't mean I've forgiven myself or trust myself with someone's heart."

The next few hours were spent mostly in silence, although that was only on the outside. Inside my head, there was so much noise I wanted to scream to make it stop.

Megan woke up from the surgery feeling groggy but impressed with the big cast on her leg. She wanted to show it to all her friends from her elementary school. I promised I'd visit her tomorrow and then gave Harrison a lift home.

I was just stepping through the front door when my phone rang.

My first thought was Indy, but even though I'd told him the reason I needed to leave, after my talk with Harrison, I couldn't deny that I'd be lucky if he ever talked to me again, let alone call me.

"Hey, Old Man," my brother said as soon as I answered.

"Hey, Kiddo."

"How's it going? Indy said your goddaughter was in an accident. Is she okay?"

"She's good. Out of surgery and rocking a cool leg cast. I reckon she's gonna milk her dad for all the ice cream in the world now."

I heard him smile on the other side of the line.

"Tate—"

"Tristan, I...I think I should probably step down from the wedding. I don't think I'm the right person to be up there with you."

I could have cut the silence with a knife until Tristan spoke.

"Is this because of yesterday? I wasn't offended, Tate. I guess I already had a feeling that you're not the biggest fan of weddings."

"I'm sorry about that. If it makes any difference, I think you and Ben are the real deal, and you're going to be happy forever. My issues are solely about me and my history with relationships."

"I wish you'd talk to me, Tate. I'm so happy to have you in my life again, but I feel you're holding back like I'm going to do something to betray you. Tate, we're not mom and dad."

I let out a choked laugh. "I'm more like him than you know, Tristan. That's why I think you deserve to have your special day with your friends around you."

"I will because I do have great friends, but I also want my family there, and you're it. You're all that's left. And I don't want you there just to fill the family gap. I want you there because you're my brother, my twin, the part of me that I always miss when you're not around."

My throat threatened to close up and my eyes watered. All I'd ever wanted was my relationship back with my brother, and here I was screwing it up.

"I'm sorry, Tristan. It's been a long, weird day in so many ways, and I'm all over the place. If you can forgive my momentary lapse in brain function, then I'd love for this conversation to reset back to when we were talking about my goddaughter."

He laughed. "So, your goddaughter. Want to tell me about her?"

We talked about Harrison and Megan for a long time until Tristan had to join the rest of the guys for dinner. They were traveling back from Vegas in the morning.

"Hey, Tristan."

"Yeah?"

"Um... how's Indy? I bet he's glad to have the suite all to himself," I said, doing my best job of sounding like I wasn't interested in the answer.

"He stayed in his room all day. Looks like the hangover hit him hard, which is not surprising. His normal routine is a lot more subdued than what you guys got up to last night."

I mirrored Tristan's laugh, glad that it seemed no one knew about Indy and me. Maybe one day the truth would come out, as it always did, and I'd face judgment, but today I was happy that there was at least one relationship I hadn't screwed up totally.

INDY

"Christ, Jake, is this the hottest September known to mankind or what?"

Jake and I were in the big kitchen of the Lexington-Bennett estate finishing the wedding cake. All around us were people busy with final preparations for Ben and Tristan's wedding.

The atmosphere was happy and electrifying if it wasn't for the heat that could destroy the work I'd spent the best part of a month planning.

"Wasn't the caretaker trying to find a generator for the walk-in refrigerator?" Jake asked just as Connor walked in.

"Wow, Indy, that cake looks stunning. Remind me to talk to you when James and I get married."

Connor was Hannah's brother and only months ago, he reconnected with his old childhood friend, James Lexington-Bennett, the owner of the estate. We'd all gone to school together, and I was really happy that they'd found each other.

"And when is that?" I asked.

"Yesterday, if he had a say in it," Connor said with a chuckle. "Anyway, let me go find Rupert. He called to say he got the generator running, so we need to hook it up to the refrigeration unit. As soon as it's all up and running, you can move your stuff in there.

"Okay, boss, what else is there? Do you want me to get started on the cupcakes?"

"Yes, please, Jake." I looked at the clock on the wall. "I'm going to check in on Ben and will be back in ten."

I knocked on the door of the room where Ben was getting ready and went in. Ellie was tying the knot on his tie while Charlotte slept peacefully on a blanket on top of the bed.

"How's the groom to be?" I asked.

"He's a pile of nerves, and someone needs to slap it out of him," Ellie said. "I would, but I don't want to set a bad example for my child."

I went over to the bed. "Can I just stay in this room for the rest of the day staring at this gorgeous specimen of a human being?"

"Nope, someone needs to be right up there with me in case I faint when I see Tristan in his wedding suit," Ben said.

"Is your dad still walking you down the aisle?" I asked.

"Yeah. I know it sounds so old fashioned, and I wasn't going to do it, but when we told him about the wedding, it was the first thing he said. I hope it's not awkward for you going in from the side."

I caressed Charlotte's chubby cheek and smiled. "I think it's great. I'm still plotting the demise of my entire family since they sent me a year's supply of dick chocolate chips, and it's not like I'd get married, but if I did, I'd love for my dad to walk me down the aisle."

Ben looked at me and then came over and sat on the other side of the bed. He looked adoringly at his daughter. There was no question that Charlotte had Ben's cute nose and chin.

"Indy...um, did something happen between you and Tate?"

I got up from the bed and looked at my non-existent watch. "No? No, of course not, why do you ask? I should get back to the kitchen. I'll check in on Reed, too, to make sure the flowers are perfect."

"I'm sure they will be. It's okay if you don't want to talk about it, but you know you can, okay?"

"Okay."

I left the room and looked for the nearest bathroom, which was right across the room where Tristan was getting ready. I closed the door behind me and flipped the lock.

Over the last week as the wedding date approached, I'd had several pep talks with myself. I hadn't seen Tate since Vegas, and our communication was rare and not exactly flirty.

There had been no more joint movie nights or late-night phone calls. One night and a drunken mistake were all it took to obliterate our friendship to dust.

I missed him, and not just the man that burrowed inside my heart and refused to leave. I missed my friend.

One fucking night.

I now wished I hadn't wanted to go dancing. I wished I'd never dared to join that queue to the bar or talked to the other couple. I wished for time to go back.

I took a deep breath and washed my face with some cold water.

In just an hour, two of my best friends were getting married, and that really made my heart happy. I remembered when Ben, who was a couple of years younger than me, had got his glasses. Everyone at school teased him, but I thought he looked really smart and cool and I told him that.

I remembered the night just over a year ago when a clearly in love Tristan had waited for Ben's event at Bookmarked to finish so he could go and sweep him off his feet.

One drunken night and Tate and I hadn't made it. We were clearly not meant to be, even when sex was all that was on the table.

The only problem was that as far as I knew, we were still married, which was reason enough to make me laugh out loud. Somehow in our drunk state, Tate had used his address on the form so the marriage certificate would be posted to him, and in his few replies to my messages, all he'd said was that he hadn't received it yet.

My phone rang, and I saw Tom's name on the display.

"Hey, Tom."

"Where are you hiding? I'm coming for you, and I have supplies," he said.

I laughed when really I wanted to cry for having Tom in my corner and said. "Bathroom upstairs."

"I'll knock three times."

A moment later, there were three knocks on the door.

"You know," I said, opening the door. "You could have just called for me."

"But that wouldn't be as exciting as pretending I'm a secret agent about to give you a super disguise. No one will ever recognize you," he said, placing a bag next to the sink.

"What's that?"

"Makeup, my dear. No one will ever know you've locked yourself in a bathroom crying for hours over the love of your life."

I scratched my hair and re-tied my bun.

"Tom, I've been here for literally ten minutes, and I haven't been crying."

"Oh, you will when you see how sexy that hunk of a man looks in a Fabulize bespoke suit, which reminds me...when are you getting dressed?"

"Um, I don't know, now? I was working on the cake and didn't want to get dirty."

Tom opened his bag to show the biggest assortment of makeup I've ever seen outside of Sephora.

"I'm not wearing make-up."

"Really? Not even a little bit?" he asked. I shook my head. "Fine, you'll wear a pep talk instead. Now sit down."

I did as he said, figuring that it was better to obey and

listen to him than challenge him and end up leaving the bathroom with mascara and foundation on my face.

"Listen to me, Indy. You are stunning. You rock that man bun like you're sex on legs, and the way the color of your hair matches your eyes would have Coco rising from her grave to applaud your sense of effortless style."

I smiled at him, happy that he had Wren in his life because he was such a special person and deserved all the love there was.

"Tom, thanks for the pep talk, but I've never had issues finding willing guys. They're just not willing to date me or ready to fall in love with me."

"That's where you're wrong."

"What?" How was I wrong? Did I miss the queue of lovers willing to propose outside my coffee shop? I didn't think so.

"Indy, you're blind if you don't know that Tate is in love with you. Even before this crazy idea you two had of getting married in secret, I could tell. All the questions he asked about you. The looks when he thought no one else was watching. And don't get me started on the sexual tension when you two are in the same space."

Tom had been the one I'd confided in after Tate had left Vegas. He made excuses for me so I could hide away in my room until we came back home.

Now that he was being a smart ass, I wasn't too sure it had been a good idea.

"And somehow, I'm still here. Single and waiting to find out if my marriage has been annulled." I sighed. "I just need to get through today and make sure Ben and Tristan have the best wedding. Then I'll go home to eat dick chocolate chip cookies and lick my wounds."

"*D*o you remember that time we went camping with Dad?" Tristan said, buttoning up his dress shirt.

"The one and only?"

"The one and, thank fuck, the only," he said, laughing.

I straightened his shirt collar over his tie and started working on the knot.

"What about it?"

"Do you remember how we couldn't get a fire going, and he forgot to bring food because he thought there would be a shop nearby?"

I did remember it. It was the last happy memory I had with our dad.

"We ended up getting back in the car and driving ten miles to a side-of-the-road grocery store that looked like out of a horror movie," I said.

"And then Dad couldn't find his way back to the campsite."

I stopped and looked at Tristan. "I had a great time that night. God, do you remember all the candy he let us eat, promising we'd tell mom he caught a big fish and ate it for dinner?"

"We didn't even have fishing rods." He shook his head.

"Sometimes I wish we were back there, you know?" I said. "That time when we were a family."

Tristan put his hands on mine and squeezed them. "If there's one thing I learned since, it's that family is what we make. Sometimes it's hard work, and sometimes it's the most natural thing in the world."

"When did you know Ben was your family?" I asked.

He smiled. "The day we met I knew there was something special about him. But it's all the days that came after that. Every day I find new things that explain the feeling I had on that first day."

"Like what?"

"Like when he wears my cologne so he can smell me all day. How he leaves little messages on sticky notes inside the books I'm reading. How he wakes up every morning and it's like he's still happy that I'm there with him. He's my everything, Tate."

"Damn, Kiddo." I let out a choked laugh.

Outside the big manor house, there was a hub of activity. I'd seen people walk back and forth with chairs, flowers, and food.

My brother was having his dream wedding thanks to the help of all his friends; his new family.

He'd always been so much braver than me. He jumped on opportunities, and he was fearless.

I held on to the past too easily, using it as my compass to navigate my world.

And how's that working for you, Tate?

"Tate."

"Yes?"

"You know that twin thing we used to have? It hasn't gone away, you know?"

"What do you mean?"

"I mean that you're hurting, and I can feel it."

I walked to the window and stared out. My breath caught when I saw Indy. He looked stunning in his gray slacks and white shirt with the sleeves rolled up, his hair tied up in that perfect messy bun.

He looked around and then pointed at various locations beyond my line of sight. It was followed by Reed and a couple other guys carrying lavender arrangements.

"He's a really good guy, Tate."

"What?"

"Look, I don't know if something happened between you and Indy, or if you just want it to happen, but I'm just saying, he's a good guy. Indy puts everyone first all the time. We can't plan an evening out without one of us guarding the door to Spilled Beans to stop his customers from coming in after hours."

"Why?" Indy had never mentioned anything before.

"There's a rumor that he's a love doctor, but in reality, he's just very good at listening. People go in when they know they won't be interrupted. They tell him what's wrong, and he listens, then he gives you the kind of advice that is so obvious you kick yourself for not thinking of it first," Tristan laughed as if he had first-hand experience.

I sighed. "He's too good for me."

"That's interesting," my brother said, sitting on the sofa by the window and looking at his wristwatch.

"What is?"

"Ben told me about your conversation when he had the exact the same doubt. You see, Big Brother, whether or not we feel that someone is too good for us, it's not our decision to make."

"There are things about me he doesn't know, Tristan."

"Then tell him, and he'll make an informed decision. But sometimes it doesn't matter. What you build together is stronger and more important than the things you build when you're apart." He gave me a pat on the shoulder and a squeeze.

When had he become the big brother?

"Come on, Kiddo. Let's get you married before we have to get a walker for you to walk down that aisle."

He laughed. "I'd still be marrying the same man."

My brother's words stayed with me as we walked out toward the archway by the pond where the ceremony was being held.

The music started as Ben walked with his arm around his dad's. His sole focus was on my brother as if they were connected by something invisible but more powerful than any other force on earth.

Indy stood by Ben as soon as his dad took his seat next to his mom.

If I thought he looked good from a distance, now that he was only a few feet away from me, he looked...every inch like the man I'd fallen in love with.

He raised his eyes slowly as if he was afraid to look at me. Our eyes met, and in that moment, as the celebrant started the ceremony, it was as if there was no one else around. No grooms, no guests, just us.

The air smelled of lavender, and I could swear I heard bees somewhere in the distance.

Indy's lips raised in the smallest of smiles, but it was enough to wrap around my heart.

I looked at my brother and forced myself to pay attention to the ceremony.

Maybe Tristan was right and I should tell Indy the truth, but what difference did it make when I didn't trust myself to not hurt Indy? After all, I'd done it to Harrison.

The celebrant declared the grooms as husband and husband, and within seconds, there was a loud cheer from all the guests. Everyone made a line to greet them and give their congratulations.

I saw Indy disappear into the house followed by Jake.

There was part of me that wanted to chase after him, but a

bigger part that was shit scared and wanted to run, so I walked back from the group assembling for photos and toward the path that ran along the pond.

Only a few yards away, I saw Hannah, Ellie, and baby Charlotte sitting on a blanket. I'd met them earlier when I'd arrived and got lost in my search for the room where Tristan was getting ready.

"Hi, Tate," they said at the same time and then started laughing, which made Charlotte giggle.

I crouched down near them and met Charlotte's tiny hand as she tried to reach for me.

"They're great at this age. My goddaughter was allergic to naps, but she was always in such a great mood," I said, remembering the times when I'd babysat while Harrison and Stella had some time for themselves.

"Yeah," Ellie said. "Charlotte sleeps through the night, but it's like she finds day time too exciting to sleep."

"And who do we have here?" I asked, noticing the large dog laying at Hannah's feet.

"This is Donny and his girlfriend, Bubbles," she said.

I laughed as I saw a small turtle on Donny's back.

"Um, I've learned about the birds and the bees, but I must have missed the dogs and turtles lesson at school."

Ellie laughed. "Yeah, it's an interesting dynamic, to say the least, with Donny mostly gazing lovingly at Bubbles while she bosses him around."

A laugh erupted from me. I may have missed the dogs and turtles lesson at school, but I had definitely practiced the gazing-slash-bossy activities with Indy.

"Looks like the crowd won't be finished with photos for a while, so I'll catch you later," I said, getting up to continue my walk.

It was a hot day, so the trees along the pond provided refreshing shade. I kept walking until I'd completed the circular walk of the pond, which considering the size, would be more accurately described as a lake.

I couldn't put it off any longer, so I went into the ballroom where the reception was being held. There was a long table at the end of the room for the grooms and best men. It was still empty since Tristan and Ben hadn't done their big entrance, so I located my seat and took my phone out. There was a message from Harrison.

Harrison: I want photos, a slice of wedding cake, and for you to promise you've got somewhere to stay if you drink.
Tate: Yes, dad. I'm not drinking because I'm driving home tonight, and I need to know what you're willing to forfeit for that slice of cake.
Harrison: I'll stop nagging you about your man if you bring me cake. And wtf, Tate. Weddings are for getting drunk and sleeping with the best man.
Tate: And look where that's gotten me.

I pocketed my phone just as Indy sat down at the other end of the table. There were only two seats between us, but from the look on his face, it may as well be a whole world.

INDY

I could have kissed Jake for giving me an excuse to escape as soon as the ceremony was over. The catering company had offered for us to use one of their tables, so with my help, Jake dressed the table and we placed the wedding cake on top.

The table had a fake bottom that held ice, and would make sure the cake wouldn't get too hot, and it could be on display in the reception hall instead of coming out only when it was time to cut and serve.

Thank god for all the guests that wanted endless photographs with the grooms because I made it to my table just in time to sit down before Ben and Tristan made their entrance.

The head table faced the rest of the room, so I was able to get through lunch without needing to talk to Tate. Not that I didn't feel his presence regardless, even with Tristan and Ben between us.

I should have known my luck would run out at some point, and that that point would be way before I was ready to talk to him.

He came around my side of the table and extended a hand.

"Dance with me?" he asked.

"Not sure it's a good idea because I ended up marrying the last guy I danced with. Not that I remember any of it, but I heard he was the one doing the proposal."

I heard his intake of breath and carried on because I was a little—okay, a lot—angry with him. He had no right being here looking all sexy and edible in that suit.

"Do you think I could get the marriage annulled on account that it wasn't consummated? Because, you know, after the groom found out we were married, he bolted. I mean, he could have at least given me a blowjob for the trouble, right?"

"Indy."

I looked up and saw the plea in his eyes.

"Fine," I said putting my hand on his and letting him lead me to the dance floor.

He looked like he was stopping when we reached the dance floor, but he carried on toward the doors leading to the garden.

"Where are we going?" I asked.

He didn't answer, but we finally stopped under a tree halfway between the house and the pond. We could still hear the music from inside, so he pulled me to him and kept hold of one hand while the other went around my waist.

Tate rested his head on mine and inhaled. My heart was getting tighter the longer we stood there swaying from side to side. I needed him to tell me whatever he needed to tell me so I could go.

"I'm sorry I left you in Vegas," he said.

"Your goddaughter was in an accident. You had to go."

It had hurt being left in Vegas only a couple of hours after finding out we accidentally got married, but surely he knew that I'd understand the reason he had to go.

"True, but the moment I made the decision to go was less about Megan and more about us and how I felt about what had happened."

As if my heart didn't feel small enough already.

I tried to keep my voice steady as I said, "How did you feel?"

"This is going to sound like I'm the biggest asshole in the history of assholes, but...I blamed you."

I pushed him away but his grip tightened.

"Let me go," I shouted.

"Please, Indy, let me explain."

"You can explain without touching me."

He relented and let me go. I took a few steps back and turned to face the pond.

"Go on..."

"You want a relationship, you want to get married. At that moment, my first thought was that we'd done it because you wanted to get married and we were both drunk so you took advantage."

I laughed, "You're right. You are the biggest asshole. If you're done with telling me how much this is all my fault, then I'd like to go back to my friend's party."

And go hide in the bathroom and this time really cry.

"When the cab driver told us that I proposed to you I didn't want to believe it. I didn't believe it until I remembered it. I was in the waiting room with Harrison waiting for Megan to wake up from her surgery, and it all came to me. Do you remember what I said?"

I shook my head, lying to protect my own heart.

"I guess it doesn't matter, but Indy, I was the one that started it. Drunk or not, we got married because I proposed."

"Well, I'm glad we got that sorted out. There's another thing to sort out. Do you have the annulment papers?"

I turned around when I heard a rustle of paper. Tate took an envelope from the inner pocket of his suit jacket and handed it to me.

"Good. If it's okay, I will show these to my lawyer and make sure they're filled correctly. I will be in touch when it's all finalized," I said, walking past him toward the house via the side door to the kitchen. Extra points for not turning around when he called me, and double extra points for not crying until I was safely inside the bathroom.

As soon as the door was locked, I took my clothes off, laid them carefully next to the sink, and walked into the shower before I turned the water on.

The first hit of the cold water was perfect. I swore like a sailor and laughed because that's all you can do when you realize you're in pain and it'll take a few seconds until you either adjust to the temperature or the water warms up.

Fortunately for me, this was an old house, so it took what seemed like forever for the water to warm up. Unfortunately for me, the warm water still came, and when it did, that was when my brain had nothing else to hold on to.

I sat on the floor of the shower and let all my frustration, sadness, and heartbreak leave me through my tears. When I didn't have any more tears left, I pulled my knees up to my chest and rested my head on them.

At some point, I reached out to turn the water off, but I had no idea how long I'd been in there.

My phone rang but I ignored it. The cake was all set up, and Jake was tasked with helping the grooms cut the first slice before he took over to cut the rest.

There was nothing left for me to do, so I pulled a towel from a cupboard and dried myself off slowly. I had no other speed.

I put my suit back on and then stared at my hair. This was the longest it had ever been. Spilled Beans was doing great, which meant longer days and less time off. I couldn't even remember the last time I'd had it cut.

My phone rang again. It was Tom. I declined the call and then called my mom.

"Hey, Mom."

"Hey, sweetie. How are you? How's the wedding?"

"I'm good. Listen, could I drop by next weekend for you to cut my hair?"

"Of course, you don't need to ask. Is everything okay? You sound...upset."

"No, Mom, just tired. It's been a long week."

"If you say so. Oh, I found you the perfect gift to help you relax..."

I groaned, a million things already going through my mind.

"Don't worry, I haven't bought it yet. I'd like to know your opinion first."

I laughed. "Who are you and what have you done with my mom?"

"Oh, shush. I'm sending you a link to your phone. If you want it, just ping me back a yes."

"Okay, Mom. Love you."

"Love you, too, sweetie."

A second after I disconnected the call, a message came through. I clicked on the link that took me to a website that sold plush organs, specifically a penis neck pillow.

I looked at the picture of the stuffed penis, with two little eyes and a smile. I started laughing and suddenly, I couldn't stop. When I thought I had no more tears left in me, they started running again, but this time it was different. I'd found the penis that broke the camel's back.

I sent my mom a yes in capital letters and gave myself one last look in the mirror before going back to the party.

Fuck Tate, fuck love, fuck marriages. I had the best family I could have wished for and friends who'd do anything for me. What the fuck did I have to feel sorry for?

It was time to give a best man's speech that would leave the room sobbing with laughter and drunk on love, then eat cake, drink cocktails, and dance until there was no bottom left on my shoes.

TATE

I should have felt relieved.

Indy had the annulment papers and had agreed to sign them.

No marriage, no relationship, no chance of hurting him.

So why did it feel like I'd put a noose around my neck and pulled it tight?

I looked at my watch to see if it was too early to go home.

We'd done our speeches. Indy's was beautiful. People laughed and cried, but while everyone was looking at Ben and Tristan, I'd had my eyes on Indy.

He'd recited a practiced speech. Everyone saw emotion, but I didn't hear it in his voice, and it certainly wasn't in his eyes.

The words about commitment, compromise, and love hit too close. As soon as he finished his speech, I stepped out of the hall, leaving the grooms to cut the wedding cake.

Tom came out of the house, walking in my direction with purpose. The hairs on the back of my neck stood at attention. This was it, shit was going to go down.

"Follow me or I'll tear your balls off, mash them, dry them

in the oven, grind them into glitter powder, and make tiny bars of soap out of them."

"Sounds like you've given that a lot of thought," I said, following him toward a large greenhouse on the side of the house.

Tom was always a picture of fashion perfection, so to see him ignore the amount of dirt and cobwebs in the greenhouse had to be an indication of his mood.

"Let's lay the cards on the table. I know about the arrangement you two had, and I know about the Vegas wedding. And now I want to know why my friend spent an hour crying in the shower before his speech, and is now in the bar drinking himself into stupidity, talking about dick pillows and taking his shoes off."

It had to do a double take because this was too much information all at once.

"Wait...dick...what? You knew? And...how do you know he was crying?"

"Because I walked past the bathroom upstairs to...well, that's private stuff, and it doesn't matter, but I walked past, and I heard him in the shower."

"How do you know it was him? Could have been anyone."

Clutching at straws, Tate Brooks.

"Because everyone else was accounted for in the hall. Wren was..." he coughed and blushed. "Wren was busy somewhere. Anyway, Indy was the only one I saw leave the hall with you earlier, and then he didn't pick up my call."

"Tom, I don't know what to tell you. We talked. Clarified some things, and then I gave him the annulment papers for him to sign."

"You...what?"

The little I knew of Tom had me painting a picture of someone who saw the world in color, someone who was kind, funny, and a little bit of sparkly chaos all in one tiny human-sized package.

No one warned me to never ever get on his bad side.

I couldn't help smiling and liking Tom a little bit more for how fiercely loyal he was to his friend.

"Tom, we were drunk, and we didn't know what we were doing."

"I will give you that. Marrying drunk in Vegas is the plot of a bad romance movie, but come on, are you really that blind?" he said, opening his arms as if whatever his argument was, was really obvious.

"What do you mean?"

"When are you going to wake up and smell the cinnamon buns? That man is in love with you. In fact, he loves you so much he's doing what he does with everyone. He's putting you and what you want before what he wants and what he needs."

"That's crazy," I said, shaking my head.

Tom crossed his arms and said, "Oh really? Then explain why he would agree to such a ridiculous idea like being fuck buddies, huh?"

"That was his idea."

He raised a brow.

"Because..." Fuck. "Because... he thought it was what I wanted."

Tom made a full-body *finally'* gesture, but I was too lost for words to smile.

I needed some fresh air.

The sky was getting dark. The music coming from the house had changed from slow and romantic to something pop that you could dance to.

Tom put his hand on my arm and said, "How do you feel about him, Tate?"

I loved him. I loved him so much it fucking hurt to breathe when he was around and I couldn't touch him. Not that I said it out loud, because all the words had left me.

"If you feel the same about him, go in there and sweep him

off his feet, or please let him go. Whatever you decide will dictate who will take him home, but make no mistake. He's not spending the night alone."

I got the message loud and clear.

"Tom, I'm going to need your help."

He screeched and jumped up and down, giving me a really awkward hug.

"Calm down, Twinkle Toes," I said, laughing.

I took a deep breath and walked back to the hall where the tables had been cleared to make space for a bigger dance floor.

Even if my body wasn't attuned to Indy, I'd know where he was straight away, because right in the corner of the large room, where the bar was located, there he was, sitting on a tall bar stool with a cocktail in his hand, and...barefoot.

I approached carefully.

"Oh, there he is. My loving husband," Indy said in a semi-slurred speech. His body swayed with every move of his arms. There were a few women with him that I hadn't been introduced to, so I figured they weren't close relatives of Ben.

"Isn't he gorgeous, girls?"

I felt all eyes on me and moved closer to Indy.

"Oh, shhhhh, that's right, no one's supp...osed to know." He put his finger in front of his mouth and leaned forward, almost falling out of his stool.

"Jesus, Indy. Let me get you out of here," I said, taking his arm to help him down. "Where are your shoes?"

"No! You're not the b...boss of me. Don't think just because we're married you can tell me what to do. Thatsh not how this"—he pointed between him and me—"works, alright buddy?"

The girls giggled, and one of them asked the bartender for another cocktail.

"Oh, yes please. Can I have a Sex in the Bathroom? That's *the* best cocktail," Indy said and then burst out laughing.

"That's not the name, is it? It's um...Sex in the Shower," he shouted.

A few more people looked over our way, so I knew I had to cut this short before he made a bigger scene. Tom had said Tristan and Ben had gone up to change into their travel clothes and would be leaving for their honeymoon to Big Sur soon. He'd cover for our absence if anyone asked.

"Wwwaait...nope, it's gone. What did you say?" Indy asked.

"Indy, where are your shoes?"

He shrugged, but another one of the girls picked them from the floor and gave them to me.

I placed one arm behind his back and another under his legs and lifted him from the barstool.

"Oh, you carried me over the threshhhhold on our wedding night...I...member now."

He wrapped his arms around my neck and said, "Are we going to consu...um...cons...con...su...mate now?"

His eyes were half-lidded, and he felt limp in my arms.

"If only you knew how adorable you are right now, Indigo Birch," I sighed as I carried him out of the house toward my car.

Tom came out holding Indy's jacket. I saw the annulment papers sticking out from the pocket. Our eyes met, and I knew what he wasn't saying. I nodded.

"Help me get him in the car."

Tom went around to the passenger door and opened it for me so I could get Indy in the passenger seat.

"I like it when you strap me in. It's kinky. Mmmayybe if you're good, I'll let you do...things...like...all the things..." Indy whispered in my ear as I buckled his seatbelt.

My dick hardened in my slacks. I groaned because there was no way anything would happen between Indy and I until we could talk, and that would require him being sober.

Indy fell asleep as soon as the car started moving and woke up when I was unbuckling him.

"Tate?" he said, his voice groggy from sleep.

"Yes, baby?"

"Where are we?"

"We're home, baby," I said, helping him out of the car.

Getting up the stairs to his apartment proved harder than I thought, but fortunately, he didn't put up too much of a fight when I helped him out of his clothes and into bed.

"Tate," he whispered.

I laid on the bed next to him over the covers and removed his hairband, massaging his scalp gently. He moaned and then went quiet so I thought he'd fallen asleep.

"If you're not a dream, please be here in the morning."

"I promise, baby," I said.

"Tate?"

"Yes?"

"I love you."

I'd heard those words once before in my life and vowed not to let anyone else say them again, ever.

I caressed Indy's beautiful face until his breathing evened as he fell asleep.

INDY

The pounding in my head wasn't as bad as I thought it was going to be, but I was still afraid to open my eyes.

My last memories were of doing my best man speech after Tate's, then eating wedding cake and going for seconds because the cake tasted fucking awesome, and then I'd gone to the bar with the purpose of getting drunk.

I couldn't attest to the rest, but the yucky taste in my mouth and the slight headache told me I'd been successful at least at one of those three things. Also the lack of memory.

Indy, you're getting too old for this shit.

Relief washed over me when I opened my eyes and saw I was home, in my own bed. Beans was closed for the next few days because I'd given myself and Jake the time off after working almost around the clock on the wedding cake and cupcakes.

I could go back to sleep and not move until the middle of next week, right?

The alarm clock on my bedside table showed it was only eight in the morning.

Fucking baker's body clock.

I sat up in my bed and reached out for the full glass of water next to the clock and the two headache pills. I gave past Indy a mental high five for pre-empting my current state.

The dick painting stared at me. I needed to get rid of it.

Right next to it were my suit slacks and shirt neatly folded with the jacket wrapped over the back of the chair in the corner. I sat up straighter and saw my shoes next to it on the floor.

Okay, even if past Indy had been smart enough to get water and pills, there was no way any version of Indy would have bothered to fold clothes that were going to the dry cleaners, anyway.

A noise came from the kitchen, and it sounded like my coffee maker.

Oh fuck, did I bring someone home last night?

Dread settled in my stomach, making me feel nauseous. I couldn't deal with kicking someone out right now. I also didn't remember seeing anyone at the wedding that I'd want to hookup with. Well, other than Tate, and there was no chance of that happening.

I opened the bedroom door quietly. From my room, I saw the living room and the kitchen, but if someone was by the coffee maker, there was no way to see them, so I stepped out of the room on tiptoes.

There was no one in the living room or the kitchen. My coffee maker was on a timer, which was why it was on, even though I didn't remember setting it, and by the looks of it, I had a fresh pot ready to drink.

I went to the cupboard, took out a cup, and filled it with coffee before sitting at the kitchen table trying to piece together whatever the hell was happening.

If I couldn't remember anything past the moment I saw Tate leave the hall after the speeches, how did I get home?

Tom!

It had to be. I finished my coffee and went back to my

room to grab the phone, remembering just in time that the rest of the world would probably get up later the morning after a party. I sent him a message instead.

Indy: Weirdest morning ever. Tell me you brought me home last night or I'm going to start believing fairies exist.

I put the phone down not expecting to hear from Tom for at least a couple of hours.

My stomach rumbled. I opened my cupboards and thanked myself that alongside my baker's body clock came an always stocked up cupboard.

I took out the ingredients I needed for my quick rise cinnamon buns and got to work.

My phone dinged with a message, but I had my hands full of flour so it had to wait.

I was just putting the buns in the oven when my doorbell rang.

"Okay, my pretties. You do your thing because daddy is hungry now," I said to my cinnamon buns, willing them to bake quickly and evenly.

I opened the door to a very confused Tom.

"Hey, sorry I couldn't answer your message. My hands were busy. Is everything okay?"

He looked behind me and then at me before he came inside.

"You're on your own?" he asked.

"Yes. Tom, did you bring me home last night?"

He furrowed his eyebrows and kept looking around.

"Are you sure you're on your own?"

"Um...pretty sure. Well, give me twenty minutes and I'll be in the company of a dozen cinnamon buns drizzled in a pornographic amount of icing. Do you want a cup of coffee?"

He nodded and followed me to the kitchen.

"So, are you my fairy godmother or what?"

"No," he said. "Indy, I didn't bring you home last night."

"Who did?"

Please don't say Tate. Please don't say Tate.

"Tate."

Fuck.

"Why?"

"You were drunk as fuck. He offered to bring you home."

"How kind of him." And now I was angry with myself because I hadn't considered that my super 'get happy' plan would mean he'd be there to watch me make a fool of myself.

I groaned, running my hands through my hair.

"So, um, you don't remember anything at all?" Tom asked.

I looked at him. "Hey, no judging."

He raised his hands. "None from me, sweetie, but talk to me about last night ..."

This required more coffee. Sadly, the timer on the oven still said I had to wait ten more minutes for the cinnamon buns.

"Tate gave me the annulment papers to sign yesterday."

"And that's why you got drunk."

I nodded. "I know this is my fault, Tom. I should have never fallen in love with him. I knew he didn't want a relationship, but my stupid heart ignored all that. And I know there's no other solution other than an annulment, but fuck, it feels like I'm so easily disposable, like we really *were* nothing more than fuck buddies. We haven't even talked about it like two adults."

Tom pursed his lips and sat back on his chair.

"Do you remember what Wren did after the baking competition?"

I did. Wren had pulled away from Tom as soon as he'd been declared the winner of the Pride Festival Bake-off. Tom had been heartbroken until Wren declared his love and they made up.

"He was protecting you. That's why he did what he did."

"Wren was protecting me from external danger. He was afraid someone would act on their threats."

I nodded, not really sure what this had to do with me and Tate.

"What if Tate is doing the same?" Tom said.

I laughed. "There's no one threatening to set my coffee shop on fire, Tom."

"No, but what if the danger isn't external, but is Tate's *perceived* internal danger?"

"What are you talking about?"

Tom got up, looking frustrated.

"For the love of Coco. Do I have to do everything around here?" He put his hands on my face and squished my cheeks until I looked at him. "What if Tate believes he's the danger? He's the one who's not good enough for you?"

I tried shaking my head, but I couldn't move it.

"No, why would he think that?"

Tom laughed. "You two are so blindly in love with each other, you can't even see it."

I snorted. "He's not in love with me."

"Oh no? Then tell me why was he all mopey after you two talked yesterday, and why do you think he brought you home and made sure you were safe?"

"I don't know. A misplaced sense of responsibility?"

The oven timer dinged, and Tom went straight for it to take the baking tray with the cinnamon buns out. They were still steaming, but he separated four buns and put them in a box he found in my cupboard and drizzled half of the icing on top. I just stood there and watched as he took over.

"These," he said, raising the open box up, "are payment for me being a super friend. I'm going home to share these with my fiancé who, if he knows what's good for him, is still naked in bed. I suggest you look at those annulment papers carefully."

He gave me a kiss on the cheek and left. It took me a minute to recover from Tom's whirlwind.

I went to the bedroom and looked for the papers I'd kept in my jacket pocket.

It was funny to think that the end of my tenuous relationship with Tate fit neatly folded in a pocket.

I unfolded the papers and sat on my bed. I read every page from top to bottom. It took me a while to find what Tom had hinted at earlier. I looked at every single page of the document again. They were all missing something.

Tate's signature.

TATE

I looked at the clock on the wall. Harrison and I had been called to this meeting by the boss because apparently, those who wanted to go somewhere in this partnership didn't care whatever day of the week it was.

Months ago, hell, weeks ago, it wouldn't have made a difference being at the office on a Sunday morning. All it would mean was that after the meeting, Harrison and I would go for a run together and then cook some steak on his back porch while enjoying a cool beer.

Now, I was seconds away from telling my boss I wasn't interested in this meeting, in a promotion, or even my fucking job.

Okay, Tate, calm down. Bills don't pay themselves.

"So, I feel this is the best strategy for the Partnership going forward. A partnership that is light at the top is more able to invest in the lower ranks where the good work is done," Andrews said.

Translation: no opportunities to move up, but we have the pleasure of adding to our workload by spending more time working with the junior attorneys.

My dream come true.

"Thank you, sir. I fully support the direction you're taking us, and I'm confident this is the most efficient route to future proof the partnership."

Harrison gave me a sideways look.

Yes, I know. My bullshit sounds like bullshit to me, too.

Another forty minutes of strategy that for the life of me I couldn't understand why it couldn't be done during the week, and we were released.

"What do you say we skip the run and go straight for steak and beer?" Harrison said as we got into the elevator.

"Not today. I'm going to come clean to Indy."

Harrison smiled and put a hand on my shoulder. "Just remember, you're not asking for forgiveness."

I nodded and gave him a heartfelt hug.

"You're an amazing man, Harrison."

"Wait, say that again. My phone wasn't recording."

We went our separate ways when the elevator doors opened in the underground parking lot.

I contemplated going straight to Chester Falls, but I was already late by hours, so it wouldn't hurt to grab a shower and some clean clothes from home.

My stomach started churning at the thought of opening up to Indy. I didn't know if I should feel hopeful or start preparing myself for rejection.

I put on sweatpants after my shower and started packing a bag. I was working remotely this week, so if all else failed, I could crash at my brother's place since they were on honeymoon.

My phone rang.

"I'm going to kill you. Like...an actual, proper death," Tom said.

"Sounds terrifying. What have I done?"

"What haven't you? Indy woke up alone. We talked earlier, but I just went to check in on him, and he's gone."

What?

"Hold on, there's someone at the door."

I opened my front door and found myself face to face with none other than the man I was in love with.

I stepped aside to let him in and gestured for him to follow me.

"Here's here."

"What do you mean, there?" Tom asked.

"Tom, he's here, and he's okay. I'll call you later."

I disconnected the call. Indy looked at me with uncertainty. He put his hands in his jean's pockets as if he didn't know what to do with them.

"I was just packing up to go back to Chester Falls," I said.

"Why?"

"Because we need to talk."

He nodded. "You took me home last night."

"I'm so sorry, I didn't want you to wake up alone, but I got a notification from work to attend a meeting this morning and had to leave."

"On a Sunday?"

I laughed, "Welcome to a day in the life of an attorney. Although I've spent the morning wondering if it's all even worthwhile."

"Why? You don't like being an attorney?"

"I love it, but the type of law I practice is affecting my life, and that's not acceptable. I'm actually considering making some changes."

"What kind of changes?"

I walked over to Indy and pried his hands from the pockets and brought them up to my lips to kiss them and then rest them on my chest.

"Can we sit down and talk? And I don't mean about my career."

He smiled and nodded, following me to the couch.

I took a deep breath and stilled myself.

"I told you about the boyfriends I had in college that cheated on me." Indy nodded. "What I didn't tell you was that I also cheated on someone really special once. I met Harrison in my first year of college. We became friends straight away, although he always wanted more. Something he told me repeatedly." I chuckled, remembering how Harrison had given me a list of reasons as to why we should be together, the main one that we already lived together.

"I liked him, like, really liked him. I was so afraid of ruining our friendship that I started dating other guys."

"The ones that cheated on you," Indy said.

"Yes. Harrison and I didn't get together until our final year of college. Just like he'd predicted, we were great together. But as he started getting more serious, I started feeling like I was trapped. I still looked at other guys and found them attractive. I wanted to act on that attraction so badly it was driving me crazy. Suddenly, I realized I was just like my dad. No matter how much he loved my mom, he couldn't help chasing other women until she was finally tired of it."

"You cheated on Harrison?"

"Yes. I went out to a bar and picked up a guy and brought him home. As soon as we got in, I regretted my decision, but then Harrison came in and saw us."

Indy narrowed his eyebrows. "So...you didn't actually do anything?"

"Not technically, but I still broke his heart. We went our separate ways and met again two years later when I joined the partnership he was working at. He'd married Stella by then and seemed happy."

"Was he?"

I smiled. "He was at the time. They're now divorced, and they share custody of Megan."

"And you became friends again."

"Yes, we did. Since then, I've been so afraid of hurting

someone else I swore off relationships. I haven't had a second date in years."

I ran my fingers from his forehead to his cheek and tucked a loose strand of hair behind his ear. "You came along with your big heart, your captivating eyes, and blue hair, and for the first time in years, I was afraid."

"Why?"

"Because I couldn't control the outcome. I couldn't stop myself from wanting more of you. Even if all we did was watch films together. But then there was more. More feelings, more desire, more...love."

A small tear fell down Indy's cheek. I wiped it clean with my thumb.

"Why didn't you tell me?"

"Because I was afraid. What if you fell for me and then I started looking at other guys? What if I hurt you?"

"It was already too late, Tate." His eyes filled with more tears. "I already loved you. I was happy to have you as a friend, if that was all you wanted, but...you discarded me so easily. It was as if our friendship meant nothing to you. All because of a drunken mistake."

I couldn't stop myself from pulling Indy into my arms.

"Oh, Indy, you are definitely not easy to discard. You've wrapped yourself around my heart so tight, I don't think I can tell which part is mine and which is yours."

Our lips met with the urgency of someone who needed to take a breath and had been underwater for far too long. I'd been underwater all my life, and I needed to breathe.

Indy tasted sweet and salty, like summer and autumn, and I wanted him like I'd never wanted anyone else before. Not any of my ex-boyfriends or even Harrison.

"Indy." I pulled my lips away from his and gazed into his eyes. "I don't want to be with anyone else."

"Neither do I."

"No, you don't understand. I've been afraid all my life of hurting someone or not being faithful and being too much like my dad, but I'm not." The realization stunned me so much I wasn't sure if I should cry or shout it loud enough for my father to hear it from wherever the hell he was. "All I needed was to find the right person. Harrison thought I was his, but I wasn't. And he wasn't mine, either. But you are, Indy. You are *my* person. I love you so much."

"I love you, too, Tate. I would have any part of you that you're willing to give, but fuck, I don't want to have just a part. I want everything. All of you. Because there isn't part of me that isn't yours, that hasn't been yours for months."

He pushed me down on the sofa, and with each pass of his tongue over mine, I became freer and freer of the shackles of my past because I was finally where I was meant to be.

I raised my hips, grinding against him. The soft fabric of my sweatpants was doing nothing to hide my erection. I moved my hands to the button of his jeans, but he stopped me.

"What's up?"

He sighed. "There's one thing we need to talk about before we go any further."

"Okay."

Indy sat up and removed a small stack of papers from the pocket of the jacket he'd placed on the coffee table when he came in.

"Did you read this?" he asked.

I unfolded the papers. "Yes, these are the annulment papers."

"Anything missing there?"

I looked at them again. Everything seemed in order.

"Look at the bottom," Indy said.

I looked at him. "I didn't sign them."

I'd had the papers for what felt like an eternity, and every single day, I'd failed to mail them until I had no choice but to give them to Indy in person.

I laughed. "What a great attorney I am."

"Agreed. But since you're the only one in the room I can consult," Indy said. "does this mean we're still married?"

INDY

There was a one thousand percent chance that my heart had left my body because it was beating so fast it must have flown away.

When I'd driven the one hundred and forty miles to Boston to ask Tate why he hadn't signed the annulment papers, I didn't think I'd be lying half on top of him after he'd declared his love for me, waiting for him to answer that same question.

Tate loves me. Tate. Loves. Me.

"I guess it does, Sweet Buns. We're still married," he said.

His eyes were still on the papers, and it was hard to gauge how he felt about it.

It seemed I hadn't used all my guts on turning up at his doorstep, so I asked, "Um...how do you...feel about it?"

He looked into my eyes and smiled.

"I don't like that I don't remember our wedding. I don't like that I don't remember proposing to you. I don't like all the time that we've been apart since..."

"But..."

He kissed me gently, his lips sucking on mine, and his

teeth tugging my lower lip, making me hot, needy, and only barely cognizant.

"But I am happy, so happy, that we're still married."

"You are?"

"I am, baby. You know why?"

I shook my head.

"Because now you really are mine, and I'm not going to let you go, ever."

Okay, it was official. I was floating on air. I was lighter than powdered sugar.

Tate wrapped his arms around me tighter, and that was definitely a trillion percent my favorite place of all time to be.

"You know," he said with a deep lustful voice. "I could take you up on your offer from last night."

I groaned. "Oh no, what did I say?"

"You asked me if we were going to consummate our marriage. I'm up for it if you are."

Oh, I was up for it, so *up* it was bordering on painful. I thrust my hips against his to show him just how much.

Tate sat up, so I ended up straddling him, and then he got up, taking me with him. Fuck, I loved my tree man.

"Where are we going?"

"Tour of the house," he said, claiming my mouth again.

"Can we start with the bedroom?"

"It's like you can read my mind," he said.

I knew there were still things we needed to talk about, but now wasn't the time for serious stuff. Now was the time for fun, the sexy kind of fun.

"I'm going to say this now before I lose all kind of brain-power and so you don't accuse me of tricking you into it," I said as Tate placed me in the middle of his bed, covered my body with his, and feasted on my neck, sucking the skin and making me his.

"Hmmm, what's that?"

"There's a box of cinnamon buns in my car."

He stopped and raised his head. "Why didn't you bring them up?"

I shrugged. "In case you sent me packing with the signed papers, I was going to drown my sorrows with my buns and a vat of coffee in Pike Place Market."

He jumped up, his erection tenting in his sweatpants.

"Where are you going? And why are you taking my joystick with you?" I whined.

"Me, and your joystick, are going to rescue those buns because we're not coming out of that bed for anything other than basic needs, and this takes care of at least one of them."

He pulled his sweatpants down, giving me a view of that big, thick cock I was going to have inside of me soon. "Um, you might scare the neighbors going like that."

"Just putting some jeans on, baby. These sweatpants aren't very forgiving...but you're not going anywhere, so you can get started." He put on a pair of jeans that looked even sexier on him, considering he was still shirtless, and came back to the bed hovering over me. "When I'm back, I'm going to lick you from head to toe and eat you like you're the most delicious meal I've ever had, and then I'm going to fuck you until we're fused together."

"Fuuuuck, Tate. I think I just came," I said, rolling my eyes.

He chuckled and ran his hand over my body, cupping my erection through my jeans before taking my car keys from the pocket.

"You're such a fucking tease."

"Says he who has a box of sin in his car."

As soon as Tate was out of the door, I got undressed and settled back on the bed. I stroked my cock lazily as I took my first proper look of the room.

It had all the basic things—bed, side tables, wardrobe, a chest of drawers with a few photos, which I suspected were of Tate with Harrison and Megan.

"I'm worried about that look on your face," he said, placing the box on the nightstand and getting rid of his jeans.

"I was just thinking how your walls are a little bare. They lack a little...personality. I have a—"

"You're not dumping that god awful painting on me."

"Damnit."

"Now, where were we? Oh yes, time for a snack."

He opened the box and took his time picking one of the buns.

"Open your mouth," he instructed.

I did and he fed me a piece, and then he did something that would change my experience of cinnamon buns for the rest of my life.

He raised my legs so my hole was exposed to him and smeared the icing of the cinnamon bun all over my ass. Then he took a bite of the bun and moaned.

"I bet you taste even better."

I followed the path of his Adam's apple as he swallowed his bite of the cinnamon bun. He put the rest to one side and without breaking eye contact, he licked every inch of the icing from me.

My cock was so hard it should be considered hazardous to handle.

I grasped the bedsheets as Tate licked and kissed my hole.

"Nghnn, fuck, Tate, you're killing— Oh, just like that."

"Fuck, baby, I'm never going to get tired of your sweet ass," he said before he opened me with his tongue. The sensation alone was enough to make me buck off the bed and curl my toes. "And I'm definitely not going to be able to smell cinnamon without getting a hard-on."

"Hhn, Tate!" I came so fast I couldn't even warn him, not that it would have made a difference because he continued fucking me with his tongue and licking me through my orgasm. And when I thought my body had nothing more in it, Tate replaced his tongue with his finger.

"Hey, baby. Open your eyes."

I didn't even know I'd closed them.

"Hi beautiful," he said. I smiled and pulled him in for a kiss. "Do you still want me?"

"Always, Tate, always."

Whether he meant if I wanted his cock in me now or have him forever, the answer was the same.

"Indy, I—"

"Bare, Tate. I want to feel you inside me. I was tested recently, I'm negative, and I haven't been with anyone else since. We've had plenty between us. No more, okay? No more."

He added a second finger, curling them up to touch my prostate. I'd always been super sensitive there, which was why I loved bottoming more than anything, but Tate knew just how to keep me hanging on the verge.

"I'm negative, too. I can show you my test, but are you sure?" he asked.

"As sure as I am that you are my forever." I gasped as he pushed the fingers further inside me.

Tate kissed me but didn't add a third finger.

"Stay there," he said, stretching over to grab the lube from the side table.

"Wouldn't dream of going anywhere," I chuckled.

Tate was a sight to behold. Yes, he had an amazing body, and he definitely knew what to do with it, but it was the intensity in his eyes as he finally entered me that showed me how much he loved me and made me his.

My body came alive when he touched me, so I matched his pace, stroke for stroke, thrust for thrust, until we both came with a beautiful and earth-shattering orgasm.

We lay there entangled in each other. His hands ran up and down my back, and the way he stroked my hair threatened to send me to sleep.

"Tate?"

"Yes, Sugar Buns?"

I chuckled. "This would be the time when you tell me your bed is either self-cleaning or you have another room we can sleep in because I'm not sure I can move."

He laughed and his chest rumbled under my head.

"Come on, let's get you cleaned, and then we can move to the spare room."

"Hey, Tate? Do you have bare walls in your spare room, too?"

He slapped my ass and then carried me to the bathroom.

TATE

S ix months later

"Hey, partner," Hannah said, coming inside our shared office with Charlotte.

"Hello, beautiful," I said to Charlotte. "And look at you walking like a big girl."

Charlotte reached out for one of the chairs and insisted on making her way over to me.

"Ta. Ta," she said, raising her arms when she got to me.

I picked her up and sat her on my lap.

"You're getting really good at that, aren't you? I bet mommy and momma really love dying their grey hair."

Hannah laughed and sat down on the chair in front of my desk, letting out an exhausted sigh.

"She can't be Ben's kid because I can't see him running around all day, and god knows I haven't got the energy, so I'm blaming Ellie. And I'm getting a divorce."

I laughed. In the last six months since I'd moved to Chester Falls, I'd gotten to know Hannah and Ellie better. So much so that I'd opened an office with Hannah, specializing in family law.

Together we'd made it work for us and our families. Granted, my family was just Indy and me, but we made time for each other. No more eighty-hour weeks, no more clients who made demands based on their net worth rather than what they actually paid for the service.

"Do you mind looking after her for ten minutes? Ellie should be finished at Bookmarked soon, and I need to go to Mason's before they close to grab a few things for Charlotte's birthday party on Saturday."

"Sure. She can help me draft these contracts. Right, Pumpkin? You're going to be a big girl soon so you can help Uncle Tate."

"Ta. Ta."

Needless to say, no work got done, but I spent time spoiling my niece, and as soon as Ellie picked her up, I closed the office and went over to my favorite coffee shop.

"We're closed," Indy said from the kitchen.

"Even for me?" I asked.

He came out of the kitchen and leaned against the door. His hair was messy with white streaks from flour or sugar, and he never looked more perfect to me.

"Well, you see, I was hoping you could help me. People on the street tell me you're the heart doctor."

"Some people are beyond help," he snorted. "What is your problem, sir?"

"Sometimes I do things and I can't remember that I've done them."

"Must be a terrible ordeal. What kinds of things specifically?"

I walked to the counter and ran my finger over the top. "One time, I declared my feelings to the love of my life, but I've forgotten it all."

"How terrible. And how does the love of your life feel

about it?"

I put a finger on my chin. "Um, well...he also has his own memory problems, you see. But I am convinced that he remembers this particular occasion but refuses to tell me."

"Hmm, and how exactly do you think I can help you with your lack of memory?"

I walked over to him and ran my hands over his hair, tilting his head up.

"I thought maybe I could practice my speech on you, and you could tell me if my love would like it."

He narrowed his eyes but nodded.

I pushed him back so he'd go into the kitchen, and then lifted him up so he sat on one of the clean counters, opening his legs so I could get between them.

In that position, Indy was a little taller than me, so he put his hands on the side of my neck.

"Go on..."

I cleared my throat and looked into his blue eyes.

"One night, many moons ago, an attorney from Boston was feeling nervous about seeing the brother he hadn't seen much of growing up. He thought that to calm his nerves he'd go on his handheld device and ask if someone wanted to be friends. He was expecting it would only last one night, but much to his surprise, his friend of one night kept appearing in his life, over and over again. The attorney became enamored with this young friend, the baker, and not only because he had the best, tightest buns in the world."

Indy slapped my shoulder, but I could see the emotion in his eyes. I swallowed and carried on.

"Whenever the attorney and the baker met, everything was magical, but the problem was that neither knew how powerful they were and how their magic affected the other."

Indy's eyes became red. Fuck, if he cried, I'd cry.

Keep it together, Brooks.

"The two men hurt for a while until a well-intended friend

with remarkable fashion sense helped them set the record straight. One day, with the help of the yummiest batch of cinnamon buns, the two men made up, but there was still a problem."

"What...what was the problem?"

"The attorney couldn't remember those really important things he'd said to the baker. So he decided to think of new ones he could say that he would never, ever forget. And so, as he looked into the eyes of his beautiful baker that happened to look deliciously stunning with streaks of white flour all over his blue hair, he would say...'Indigo Moonshine Birch, I thought love was something other people felt until I met you. Even through all the hurt, you still have the capacity to love everyone and not ask for one thing in return. So I'd like to ask you this question. Will you let me give you all that love back for the rest of our lives? Indy, my love, will you marry me, again?'"

Tears ran down his cheeks, and he nodded fiercely before he kissed me. He tasted like he always did—a little sweet, a little cinnamony, and a little salty.

I pulled two engagement bands from my pocket and put one on his finger and one on mine. I'd spent weeks with a jeweler deciding on a ring that was special to us, and in the end, he helped me design a white gold band with an inset lavender flower made of amethysts.

"Oh my god, Tate, these are beautiful," he said.

"They're only a physical representation of us. We don't need it, Indy. We know who we are and who we belong to, but this way the world will know it, too."

"Put your clothes on, it's freezing out here and we're coming in," Ben shouted from the door.

"What's going on?" Indy asked.

"We're having an engagement party."

Ben, Tristan, Tom, Wren, Connor, and James all appeared, holding enough alcohol to drown a ship.

Indy hugged me so fiercely he came off the counter, but I caught him like I would every time. And I'd keep him safe from hurt and all the rest of the things that I still needed to think about for our wedding vows.

Technically we were already married, but we'd both earned the celebration. So we'd have the engagement party, the wedding celebration, the honeymoon, and especially, the happy ever after.

~

Thank you so much for reading *How to Catch a Bachelor*, the fourth book in the Chester Falls series. Keep reading to get a special bonus scene.

Up next is *How to Catch a Biker*. We met our romance author Aiden in *How to Catch a Rival* and he made another appearance in How to Catch a Bachelor. Do you think it's his turn for a HEA? You bet!

Things aren't going exactly Aiden's way right now. An asshole ex and writers block are getting him down. When he seeks the help of a silver fox biker to research for a book, guess whose engine gets revved to the max?

Be sure to follow me on Bookbub to be notified of new releases, and look for me on Facebook for sneak peaks of upcoming stories.

Please take a moment to write a review of *How to Catch a Bachelor*. If you leave a review Indy will bake you a box of his best cinnamon rolls.

If you would like to be the first to know when my new releases are available, read exclusive FREE stories and know what I'm up to, please sign up for my newsletter, Ana's VIP Readers: *bit.ly/AnaAshley*.

For giveaways, sneak peaks, ARC opportunities and general caffeinated fun times, please join my facebook group! Café RoMMance - Ana's Reader Group.

BONUS SCENE

WEDDING DAY...THE SECOND ONE

INDY

Bready or not, I'm marrying the shit out of you tomorrow.

Everything I brew, I brew it for you.

I can't espresso how much you bean to me.

You're such a weirdough.

I loaf you, you butter believe it.

I always knew we beelonged together.

We were meant to bee.

I'll see you tomorrow, husband. Love you.

Tomorrow can't come too soon. Love you back.

. . .

I forced myself to put my phone down after reading our message exchange for the hundredth time since last night.

Whoever suggested that people getting married shouldn't see each other the night before the wedding was clearly single and had never been in love.

And because we hadn't done things right the first time around, Tate had insisted we spend the night apart.

So here I was, in Reed's office, getting ready to marry the love of my life and missing him like I hadn't seen him in years rather than twelve hours.

"Knock, knock," my mom said, coming in. "Oh, Indy, sweetie, you look..." She stopped and ran a finger under her eye.

"Oh, Mom, don't cry. No crying allowed, okay? Because then I'll cry, and when Tom comes back, he'll cry, and you know all hell will break loose," I said, pulling her in for a hug.

"I'm just so happy for you, you know. Tate is perfect for you."

I nodded in her embrace.

"Do you remember when you said the wind was changing? Mom, Tate didn't come because the wind changed. Tate *was* the wind," I said, remembering the words I hadn't taken seriously when she'd said them over a year ago.

"Please let me make an inappropriate comment right now, or I'll burst into tears," she said.

I laughed. "You never asked permission for it before."

She shrugged, and then her expression changed. *Oh no.* I knew that face. My heart rate increased, and my palms became sweaty.

"Indy, dear, Tom said you already have something old, something borrowed, and something blue, so I wanted to give you something new."

Please let it not be a dick. Please let it not be a dick.

She took a small velvet box from her handbag and gave it to me.

My hands shook as I opened the box to reveal a silver boutonnière with a tiny dick charm at the end of it.

I laughed. The dick was small enough that anyone would need to be close to me to see what it was, and I knew it would be mostly hidden by the small bunch of lavender.

"Do you want to do the honors?" I asked, pointing at my lapel.

My mom looked at me with the same pride, tenderness, and love in her eyes she had when I baked my first cake, when I graduated from high school, and when I opened Spilled Beans. Being on the receiving end of that look was one of the best feelings in the world.

"There," she said, pinning the small lavender flowers with the dick-adorned boutonnière. "Looks perfect."

"I agree."

"I'm going to find your dad and your brother before they cause any trouble outside. I'll see you when you're a married man," she said, kissing my cheek.

"I'm already married," I chuckled.

She waved her hand and left the room.

I walked over to the window to look at the beautiful landscape of Reed's lavender farm. It had been Tate's idea to get married here, and Reed had been beyond excited to host our wedding, especially since the lavender-honey party favors for Ben and Tristan's wedding had been such a success.

Hushed voices outside Reed's office caught my attention. I walked out and saw Tom and Ben.

"Everything okay out here?" I asked.

Tom looked at me as if I'd shone a bright light in his face.

"What's the matter? Is anyone allergic to bees? Or is there a problem with the catering? Jake has all the contacts, and he made me promise I wouldn't get involved."

Tom looked at Ben again and then at me.

"Um...let's go inside Reed's office," he said.

"No. Tell me what's going on. Is Tate okay?"

"Um...that's the thing, we...um...can't find him."

I wanted to laugh, but Tom looked like someone had called his cat a bad name.

"Are you serious?"

He nodded, looking like he was about to cry.

"Hold on a moment," I said, returning to the office to grab my phone. I tapped on the phone finder app, and sure enough, my man had not disappeared. He'd simply...evaded Tom.

I chuckled. "I'll go look for him, okay? I promise you'll have two grooms under the lavender arch in one hour."

"Ugh, this is too much. I've changed my mind. Wedding planning is too stressful. I'll stick to making clothes. Clothes don't go missing," Tom said, running his hands through his hair and walking off. "I'm going to find Wren. I need a healing blowjob."

Ben snorted. "He did just say that, didn't he?"

I nodded. "He does make a good point though. I'll see you in one hour...oh, the office will be free if you need...you know...some healing." I snorted and walked out the door leading to the lavender field.

I didn't need to look twice at my phone to know exactly where he was.

"Did you know you scared the sparkle out of Tom with your escape?" I asked, approaching the water tower. I started going up the stairs.

"No, you can't come up," Tate shouted.

I chuckled and carried on until I was at the top.

"We're not supposed to see each other before the wedding," he insisted.

"Are you forgetting we're already married?" I walked over to him, and as always, he opened his arms and wrapped them around me. "I missed you last night. Let's not do that again."

I pulled his head down for a kiss. He tasted of Tate, coffee, and cinnamon. My all-time favorite combination. His lips on mine were now as familiar as breathing, but it didn't make each kiss any less exhilarating. If anything, every time Tate touched me, kissed me, or looked at me like I was his whole world, it was as if it was the first time.

"I agree," he said. "You look breathtaking."

He ran a hand over my hair. I hadn't decided whether I should wear it in a bun, so it was still loose.

"Why are you hiding?" I asked.

"Tom was a little overwhelming. He even gave a speech where he threatened my balls *again* if I ever hurt you."

I moved my hand slowly downward until I cupped his growing erection.

"Indy..."

"Don't worry, baby, I'll protect your balls," I said in my best sultry voice. I mean, we were on our own, we had some time, and we could totally have sex right now, right?

Tate tugged on my hair, which had the effect of diverting all my blood flow right down to my dick.

"You're playing with fire, baby," he said.

"I'm so ready to get burned. It's unreal." I removed my hand from his crotch and pressed against him so he could feel how hard I was.

Tate laughed but put a few inches between us. "How about we go out there, get married—again—take some photos, and eat nice food?"

"But—"

He kissed me until I forgot what day it was and then said, "I want to spend tonight licking lavender honey from your ass until you come. And when you do...twice...I'm going to fuck you until you come a third time."

I shivered in anticipation and then pulled his hand toward

the stairs. "Come on, we need to get this over with. How long do you think we need to stay?"

Tate laughed and pulled me until I landed with my back to his chest. He nuzzled my neck and then sucked on my skin. Definitely, one hundred percent, leaving a mark.

"Ugh, Tate...you're not helping."

"Indigo, baby. Let's slow down and enjoy today. We have the rest of our lives ahead of us, and I promise I'll make it so good for you."

I sighed, "God, Tate, that sounds...like a dream come true."

He turned me around to face him. "It's more than a dream come true, Indy. I never dared dream that my life could be like this. I never dared dream that someone like you could love me."

A silly tear left the confines of my tear ducts. I knew Tate and I were perfect for each other because even though we'd started off from different places, we both wanted the same thing. Even if we hadn't realized that in the beginning.

"Come on, you romantic sap, let's get ourselves married...again."

"I'd marry you every day for the rest of my life."

"I'll say yes, every single time."

And as I promised Tom, two grooms were under the lavender arch within the hour. And this time, we'd both remember every single detail. Walking together down the improvised aisle and seeing our closest friends and family smiling at us, witnessing the second most important moment of our lives. The most important being the moment we'd decided we were stronger together and could defeat all the hurt and doubt from our past.

TATE

"Congrats, old man," my brother said, hugging me.

"Thanks, kiddo."

The old Tate would have been itching to leave. Hell, the old Tate wouldn't have been caught dead at a wedding, let alone as the groom.

New Tate, however, couldn't be prouder to stand in front of an amazing group of people, declaring his undying love for Indigo Moonshine Birch, now Brooks.

"If you want me to cover for you, just say the word," he said into my ear.

I laughed. "I might take you up on it, but after food. Have you seen the menu Indy put together?"

"Ben hasn't shut up about it since we got here, so yeah. You can kidnap your groom any time after lunch."

Indy was talking to his brother, Sage, under the shade of a tree. I made my way toward him, which took much longer than I thought because everyone wanted to congratulate us on the wedding, the choice of venue, the sunny day, and anything and everything they could think of.

I wondered, not for the first time, if I could take my brother up on his offer to cover for us so I could take Indy away for some naked fun.

"Oh, Tate, darling, there you are," Indy's mom said, coming over to me.

"Hi, Pamela," I said, giving her a kiss on the cheek. "Can I recruit you?"

She laughed. "What for?"

"I want to get to your son, but it seems today, of all days, everyone is keen on keeping us apart."

"It's funny you should say that because I wanted to speak to you both," she said with a smile I was coming to know very well.

Oh no!

She wrapped her arm around mine and guided us to Indy, stopping anyone from getting closer by sending them toward the buffet area, where lunch would be served shortly.

Damn, why didn't I think of that?

"Oh, hey, Mom," Indy said as we approached. "Is the buffet ready yet? I'm starving."

Pamela looked at Sage, who snorted.

Indy sighed.

"Mom, I got married with a dick on my jacket, surely—"

"What?" I interrupted. What the hell was he talking about?"

Indy pointed at his boutonnière. I couldn't see it at first, but then I couldn't unsee it.

"That was there the whole time?" I asked.

"Apparently, it's my 'something new,'" Indy said with air quotes.

Pamela cleared her throat. "That was your ceremonial gift. I want to give you your *wedding* gift."

I held my hand up.

"Is it a dildo, a butt plug, a cock ring with tiny dicks all around the ring, or those delicious dick-shaped chocolate chips?" I asked.

Pamela opened her mouth wide and closed it again, so I continued, "Because Indy has the only dick he'll ever need for the rest of his life, so we'll accept a gift from the aforementioned useful-gifts list. Otherwise, I'm sure Sage will be glad to be on the receiving end of your generosity."

Sage laughed, and Pamela put a finger over her mouth as if she was deep in thought.

"Oh, I know what else you can add to that list. How about cinnamon-flavored lu—"

"La, la, la," she sang, covering her ears with her hands and walking away. Sage followed her toward the buffet area.

"How interesting your mom isn't shocked knowing we'd like new sex toys but draws the line at the thought of me eating your ass," I said, pulling Indy into my arms. "And finally, I've got you. I thought I was going to have to kidnap you for real."

"I'd be up for that. Just saying."

I smiled. "And I think that's the end of inappropriate dick-gifting, baby."

He patted my chest, shaking his head. "Oh, honey, it's like you don't know my family already?"

"I love your family, and I love you even more," I said.

Indy melted into my arms and pulled me down for a kiss. "I need your pant-dropping, brain fog-inducing kisses because I need to forget what just happened. Like, total erasure."

I chuckled but did exactly as requested. I ran my fingers through Indy's long, soft hair until one of my hands cradled the back of his neck. I caressed his cheek and looked into his dark-blue eyes.

"Anything you want, baby."

My lips had barely touched Indy's when I heard a cough behind us. Indy groaned, and I took a deep breath before looking behind me.

Tom stood there with his hands on his hips.

"I have a group of hungry people out there, and you two are over here canoodling?" he huffed, raising his hands up.

"Canoodling?" I asked, raising an eyebrow.

"I can change it to eye-fucking, but there are children present at this party," he whispered, coming closer and pulling us by our suit jacket sleeves.

We followed him until we reached the area Reed had set up for the lunch buffet. Slow, soft music was playing in the background. When I'd spoken to Reed about having the wedding at his farm, I wanted to ensure we wouldn't disturb the bees.

A roar of applause and flower petals rained upon us. So much for being considerate to the bees.

Sorry, bees.

I wouldn't have thought it was possible to feel so much happiness with one person, and here I was, with him, surrounded by our closest friends.

Maybe we wouldn't escape the party as early as we'd like.

Maybe we'd be sporting blue balls a little longer.

But as we opened the dance floor with our first dance to the sound of our song, "Lavender" by Marillion, I knew this wasn't as good as it could get. This was just the beginning.

PREVIEW OF HOW TO CATCH A BIKER

SLADE

"*H*ey, baby."

What the fuck.

I glanced at the screen on my phone to double-check that I hadn't been stupid enough to answer a call from my ex.

Unknown Number.

"Slade, honey? Are you there?" he asked in that sweet, deep voice he thought still worked for me. It had, once upon a time, many times over.

"What do you want, Mike?" I tried to keep my voice flat. I knew he'd pick on up the slightest hint of emotion and latch onto it.

"Now, now, baby. That's no way to greet your husband—"

"Ex-husband, Mike. Ex. Husband," I said, failing to take the bite out of my voice.

"That's why I'm calling," he said.

"What do you mean? And make it quick, I have work to get to."

"It's our anniversary."

"I'm hanging up."

"Wait," he said. "Please..." His voice changed, and I knew I was going to regret it, but I waited until the silence became too heavy, even for me.

"Mike..."

"I just...do you remember that day? Can you believe it was twenty-five years ago? It was so hot and sticky. The hottest day in Atlanta that summer. I was running late for work, but when I saw you, leaning against your bike wearing that leather jacket as if you were too cool to feel the heat..." he chuckled.

How could I not remember? It was the day my life changed forever, and not just for the reason he liked to remember.

"It was a good day," I confessed.

Mike's memory of the guy across the road from where he worked in his uncle's garage couldn't be further from reality.

I'd been scared and unsure. I'd wanted to cross the road and trust that the promises I'd been given weren't as empty as the tank on my trusted Harley.

Instead, I was given a job, and I'd met the man that taught me my life could be good, or at least better than it had been until then. That is until he broke my heart and my trust.

"You were always a mystery, Slade. It was exciting at first, but then..."

I sighed. "Why are we having this conversation? You were the one who left, and not before you took everything you wanted and more."

"Slade..."

"Look, I don't know what you want from this trip down memory lane, but I've moved on. I live on Reality Avenue, where I have a business to run. I suggest you go back to whatever twink you're fucking this week and leave me alone."

I ended the call before he could say anything else.

These days, the only person I kept my mouth shut for was my bank manager, so it was definitely a good idea to end the call.

It was the hottest day of the summer so far, making the

glass walls of my office feel like a fishbowl under a UV light, but Mike's interruption only delayed the work I needed to do today, so I grabbed a bottle of water from my small office fridge and drank it all in one go.

The satisfaction of closing my spreadsheets one hour later was only matched by the information they contained within. My business was doing well. So well, in fact, that maybe I could offer Liam a few more hours and consider finally taking the time to work on my bike restoration.

I stepped outside the office. Liam was in the garage working under a car and whistling a tune I didn't recognize.

The familiar smell of oil, grease, paint, and sweat calmed me down, and since there were no customers in the shop, I allowed myself the moment to enjoy the feeling of rightness whenever I was in my workspace. The garage, *not* the office. That was merely a necessary part of running a business.

When I'd seen this building only around the corner from the Chester Falls main square, I knew I'd found my perfect place.

The vintage bike shop with the adjacent garage had direct access from the main street, attracting curious passersby as well as my loyal customers.

Cars weren't really my thing, so when Liam had walked in asking for a job, just a couple of months after I'd opened the shop, I hadn't cared that I had no clue how to pay him.

As it turned out, he'd worked for the previous owners, and since there was no other garage in town, we had a captive audience. As much as I'd wanted to run an exclusive vintage bike repair and restoration shop, I knew it was smart to diversify.

I'd been dumb too many times in my life to not know when to smarten up.

The shop was exactly how I'd always wanted. Paved flooring, a few display cabinets, a leather couch, and several blown-up photos of vintage bikes on the walls.

It was big enough to have a good range of bikes on display,

mostly Harleys, but it still felt cozy and personable. Most of all, the long glass wall behind the bikes gave my customers a direct view of the garage.

"Hey, boss," Liam said, sliding out from under the car. "I put the new alternator in Mrs. Mason's car. I'll just give it a quick once over and it'll be good to go."

"That's great. Thanks, Liam. You can head home when you finish."

"You sure? I can hang around," he said, wiping his greasy hands on a rag.

"I'm sure."

"You know Maggie will bring you coffee whether or not you let me off early."

Liam was a good ten years younger than me, and after losing his first wife at a young age, he'd found love again in the girl that seemed to come by a little too often for someone who didn't own a car, bike, or even had a driver's license.

Maggie was a sweet girl in her mid-twenties, and as long as she kept bringing us coffee from Spilled Beans, she could pop by to visit Liam any time. Or have him home early as the case may be.

"I have no ulterior motive. Just being nice," I said, raising my hands.

I wasn't kidding anyone. Indy's coffee was the best and, on most days, we were so busy that Maggie's treat was a lifesaver.

"All right, then. Will we see you at the book fair later?" he asked.

I'd almost forgotten about the fair. These days, reading was my only form of relaxation, usually before I fell asleep after a long day at the shop.

"Maybe," I said. "I want to catch up on some things, but I'll drop by."

I went over to the main shop while Liam finished up. Working with cars and bikes was a messy and smelly business.

Just because the scent of oil got my engine running, it didn't mean the general public agreed with it, so I'd made sure that my staff facilities had a locker room with a shower and the best oil removing soap available.

Liam was my only employee, but the way things were going, I could see myself hiring a couple more people in the next year or so. Especially if it meant I wouldn't need to get anywhere near a car.

I glanced at the corner of the garage where my passion project stood covered up and waiting for me to get my head out of my ass and start working on it.

"All right, boss. I'll see you later," Liam said, coming into the shop area looking fresh as a daisy.

I waved him off.

"Hey, Liam," I said, just as he reached the front door. "I don't suppose you'd want to pick up a few more hours?"

He grinned widely. "You serious, boss?"

I nodded.

"Hell yeah, I'll do it. I'm saving to get Maggie a nice ring. I know we haven't been going out long, but when you know, you know. Right?"

"You can't let a girl like Maggie get away, that's for sure."

He nodded and left with the biggest smile on his face.

My mind went back to the call from Mike. I once thought we had forever too.

Saying life after my parents died wasn't easy was the understatement of the century, so when I met him, he was the ray of sunshine I craved. If he was a flower, I was a bee drunk on his sweet nectar.

Except I carried secrets I had never been able to share and, in the end, that broke us. Yes, he'd cheated, but when you hide who you really are from the person you love, aren't you as much of a cheater?

We normally didn't get many customers in the shop on

Saturday mornings, so I busied myself putting things away in the garage and closing it before heading back to close the shop.

I stole another glance at the old Harley and then pulled out the list of parts I needed to order for it. I reckoned I could have it ready by the end of the summer, when I usually closed the shop for a week to get out on the open road.

The thought alone caused my skin to erupt in excited goosebumps. I'd missed out on the trip last year, when I'd come down with an unexpected flu, so I wanted to make this year count.

I pulled out my phone and blocked the number Mike had called me from. I wasn't interested in living in the past.

The man that had saved my life said to me once, *"Slade, son, nothing good comes from looking back. Put the good memories in a safe box and move forward. Only when you're miles away from the past, can you afford to look back inside the box and pick a memory to revisit. Don't do it too early, or you'll be tempted to turn around. Make sure you're far away enough that you can't."*

Those words had carried me from Seattle to Atlanta and then to Chester Falls.

When I'd arrived in the small town six years ago, I thought I'd stepped into a place that wasn't made for people like me. It was too nice, too perfect.

Time showed me that people here were as flawed as anywhere else, and so, a day at a time, I carved out my little spot in the community.

After locking everything up, I went around the building to the outside stairs that lead up to my apartment above the store. I liked that there was a separation. My apartment was my sanctuary. There, I didn't have any secrets. I could open my memory box and bring back the good ones any time I liked.

One scan of my bookshelf reminded me that I'd recently donated some books to Goodwill, so what a perfect day to fill it up with new ones.

Maybe I'd bump into Liam and Maggie at the book fair. Maybe I'd buy her an iced coffee.

Now those were memories I wanted to make.

CONNECT WITH ANA

Connect with Ana on social media:

Hang out in my FB Group:
facebook.com/groups/CafeRoMMance
Follow me on instagram: *instagram.com/anawritesmm/*
Follow me on Bookbub: *bookbub.com/authors/ana-ashley*
Sign up to my newsletter: *bit.ly/AnaAshley*

For an overview of all of Ana's books and audiobooks, visit her website: *anawritesmm.com/books*

BOOKS BY ANA ASHLEY

Single Dads of Stillwater
A spin off series from Chester Falls that can be read on its own. Each book features one or more single dads in this community of friends, family and found family. In this contemporary MM romance series you'll find heat, emotion and a guaranteed happy ever after.
Newcomer
Antagonist
Breakthrough
Heartstring
Datebook (Coming early 2024)

Finding You Series
A standalone series set across the Atlantic between New York and Portugal. Find your way home with this contemporary MM romance series with friends to lovers, star-crossed lovers and age gap with plenty of heat, feels and always a happy ever after.
Home Again
Together Again
Love Again
And for a special short story, Complete Again, plus bonus scenes, grab the Finding You boxset now.

Room for 3 series
This is a high heat MMM contemporary romance series set in an island resort.
The Resort
The Vacation (Free short story)

Chester Falls Series
From a Prince to a Happy Ever After for all, enjoy this small town MM romance series that's as sweet as they come, with plenty of heat, humor and everything in between.
How to Catch a Bookworm (Prequel short)
How to Catch a Prince
How to Catch a Rival
How to Catch a Bodyguard
How to Catch a Bachelor

How to Catch the Boss (a Christmas novella)
How to Catch a Biker
How to Catch a Vet
How to Catch a Happy Ever After
You can now have all the books in the series and the prequel all in two boxsets.
Chester Falls Collection Volume I
Chester Falls Collection Volume II

Standalone books
Christmas Bubble: a low angst, standalone, Christmas novel featuring a petite but larger-than-life cheerleader, an older demisexual football coach and a winter cabin by the lake with only one bed. With cameos from Chester Falls and Stillwater.
Midnight Ash: a sweet Cinderella fairytale retelling with a sexy kinky twist on the side, and a cast who don't quite behave as you'd expect.
Stronghold: a sweet and sexy romance in Sarina Bowen's World of True North, Vino & Veritas series. This is a standalone story between two childhood friends who reunite after as decade apart, with some creative use of maple syrup.

FREE READS
My Fake Billionaire
The Vacation

ABOUT ANA

Ana Ashley was born in Portugal but has lived in the United Kingdom for so long, even her friends sometimes doubt if she really is Portuguese.

After getting hooked on reading gay romance, Ana decided to follow her lifelong dream of becoming an author.

These days you can find her in front of her laptop bringing her stories to life, or in the kitchen perfecting her recipe for the famous Portuguese custard tarts.

Ana Ashley writes sweet and steamy gay romance set in America, often in small towns where everyone knows everyone.

~

You can follow Ana on the usual social media hangouts.

For access to exclusive teasers, content, and general book and food related goodness you can now join Ana in her Facebook Group, Café RoMMance - Ana's Reader Group

Ana's VIP Readers - bit.ly/AnaAshley

Facebook Page - @anawritesmm

Email - ana@anaashley.com

Instagram - @anawritesmm

Bookbub - bookbub.com/authors/ana-ashley

Goodreads - goodreads.com/ana-ashley